Let s Do It Again

BOOK YOUR PLACE ON OUR WEBSITE AND MAKE THE ARABESQUE ROMANCE CONNECTION!

We've created a customized website just for our very special Arabesque readers, where you can get the inside scoop on everything that's going on with Arabesque romance novels.

When you come online, you'll have the exciting opportunity to:

- View covers of upcoming books

- Learn about our future publishing schedule (listed by publication month and author)

- Find out when your favorite authors will be visiting a city near you

- Search for and order backlist books

- Check out author bios and background information

- Send e-mail to your favorite authors

- Join us in weekly chats with authors, readers and other guests

- Get writing guidelines

- AND MUCH MORE!

Visit our website at
http://www.arabesquebooks.com

Let s Do It Again

Niobia Bryant

ARABESQUE

BET★ BOOKS

BET Publications, LLC
http://www.bet.com
http://www.arabesquebooks.com

ARABESQUE BOOKS are published by

BET Publications, LLC
c/o BET Books
One BET Plaza
1900 W Place NE
Washington, DC 20018-1211

All Kensington Titles, Imprints, and Distributed Lines are available at special quantity discounts for bulk purchases for sales promotions, premiums, fund-raising, and educational or institutional use. Special book excerpts or customized printings can also be created to fit specific needs. For details, write or phone the office of the Kensington special sales manager: Kensington Publishing Corp., 850 Third Avenue, New York, NY 10022, attn: Special Sales Department, Phone: 1-800-221-2647.

First Printing: December 2005

10 9 8 7 6 5 4 3 2 1

Printed in the United States of America

First came Ernest, then Letha, and
together they brought you and then me.
From the beginning of our time together
you have been my brother, my friend, my coach,
my defender, and even my father figure.

Thank you for teaching me about sports.
Thank you for teaching me how to fight.
Thank you for teaching me how to
stand up for myself.

To my Big Brother,
Caleb "Ab" Bryant

Love,
Pig

You are the only person I'll let call me that ☺

Prologue

"Are you sure you're satisfied with the current revisions to your will?"

Olivia Saint James's sharp eyes darted to her attorney and closest friend of the past thirty years. She never liked to be questioned, or rather, second guessed. "Why wouldn't I be satisfied with *my* own decision?" she asked.

Hampton Tyler eyed the seventy-five-year-old woman over the rim of his spectacles. "It's a rather . . . odd request, Olivia. Besides, you think it will work?"

She picked up a silver-framed wedding picture from atop her piano with a frail hand. The couple pictured there were so in love as they gazed at each other.

They had been happy . . . once. If it was up to her, and it was, as far as she was concerned, she would see to their happiness again.

"It'll work, Hamp," she told him with steely determination and a twinkle in her eyes. "When there's a will, there's a way."

Chapter 1

Five Years Later

"Marry me."

Serena Saint James looked down at the half-carat solitaire before focusing her feline ebony eyes on Zander Madison. At his expectant gaze she forced a smile to her supple lips before nervously licking them. *Where did this come from?* "Uh, Zander . . . I . . . I . . . I," she began, searching for the words to let him down easily.

His hands covered hers. "I know we've only known each other for six months, but I just feel a connection with you, Serena," Zander told her, his boyishly handsome face earnest.

Then why don't I feel it?

Zander was a wonderfully sweet man she met at the wedding reception of one of her regular clients. They talked as they danced and soon she was impressed by his ambition. He'd put himself through Hampton University and then returned to his hometown of Irvington, New Jersey, with his bachelor's degree and a teaching certificate. He now taught math at University High School in Newark.

They'd dated regularly ever since, and although a lot of women would jump at the chance to marry Zander—a handsome, educated, and employed man, Serena was not one of them. It wasn't him. It was her. Cliché, but very true. She wasn't looking for a husband and had no desire to be married. Not to him nor anyone else.

Now, how could she tell him that without hurting his feelings?

"Zander, I really care about you . . ."

"But?" he asked, his expression slightly pained.

Serena smiled softly, raising her hand to lightly caress his cheek. "But it's just too soon," she finished softly, dropping her eyes from his as she sought for an easy way out.

"Okay. That's not a yes, but it's not entirely a no either," Zander told her, grasping her hands warmly in his own.

Serena offered him no words, but she *knew* she'd never marry him.

Zander leaned forward to kiss her warmly on the mouth. Serena closed her eyes, and raised her chin to receive it, wanting that spark to *finally* ignite between them.

It didn't.

His cell phone vibrated on his belt and he broke the kiss, smiling in apology at her before answering. "Madison here."

It was ironic, but Zander's very proposal was a testament to the lack of chemistry between them. There had been no romance, or even real thought, put into his offer to spend the rest of her life with him. He didn't even wait until they were at the restaurant and dining by candlelight. Just, here's the ring, now answer the question.

The last time she'd been proposed to there had been plenty of romance and lots of tenderness, even at eighteen. She had jumped at the chance to marry her childhood best friend and first love, Malcolm Saint James. The actions of a teenage boy far outdid the dry proposal she'd just received from a grown man.

Serena thought back to nearly twelve years ago, when she thought romance and love were enough to make a marriage last. Considering that it ended in a burst of angry flames and bitter disappointment, she should've focused more on sensibility than passion.

It didn't matter anyway. Delusions of love, her failed marriage, and her ex-husband were years behind her now. No need dwelling on the past.

"Serena, that was my mother. I have to cancel dinner; there's a family emergency."

"That's okay, I understand," Serena told him, not letting him see the roll of her eyes. *Mama's boy.*

"Maybe I'll come back later on tonight," he offered, already pulling on his jacket.

It was nothing new for Mrs. Madison to just call Zander and he'd cancel any and all plans to run to her side. The last emergency was no cinnamon to go into her sweet potato pie for Sunday dinner. Never mind that Zander and Serena were on the way to the sold-out premiere of a movie. For him it was all about his mama and that damn pie. Needless to say, they'd missed the movie and instead spent the evening watching a DVD of *Big Momma's House* with *his* big mama.

Zander walked over to her and before Serena could react, he slid the solitaire onto her left finger. The weight of it was far too heavy, figuratively *and* literally.

"No, Zander—"

Tilting her head back with his finger, he kissed her full on the mouth, locking his eyes on her face. "I bought this with you in mind. Wear it . . . no strings, okay?"

Serena removed her hand from his grasp, looking down at it as she tried to pull the ring, with all its obligations, from her finger. "No. Take this—"

"See you later, baby," he hollered from across the room.

Serena looked up in surprise just as her front door slammed closed. "No . . . he . . . didn't," she exclaimed in disbelief.

Heading straight for her bathroom, Serena continued working the stubborn ring from her finger. It fit her snugly; almost as firm as the pressure Zander was putting on her to commit. *Nothing a little soap can't handle.*

Just moments later she emerged from the bathroom with damp hands now lightly scented with Lever soap and the engagement ring off her finger. The flawless diamond sparkled brilliantly in her hand as she carried it into her bedroom.

She would just have to sit Zander down again tomorrow and make it clear that his vision for their future just didn't match her own. Maybe because of those differences she should end the relationship completely. If Zander was to that point in his life where he was ready for marriage—and she knew that *she* wasn't, why keep him from finding a really great woman who wanted the same things that he did? She'd been down the road to matrimony before, and it definitely was not a trip she wanted to take again.

Opening the wooden jewelry box on her dresser, Serena's eyes immediately fell on the plain gold band snuggled against the corner of the red velvet interior. Picking it up, she compared the two rings: one simple but once cherished; the other so obviously costly, yet a burden.

Dropping Zander's ring into the box, she held

the band with her manicured fingertips. The inscription read: *Here's to infinity*.

Who knew infinity lasted just two years?

As childhood friends, Serena and Malcolm had been inseparable. As puberty reigned, and they noticed more attributes about one another besides their skills at playing video games, they both fell into the sweetness of their first love at the tender age of twelve.

First real kiss at thirteen.

Clumsy gropes at fifteen.

Third base by seventeen.

Married at eighteen.

Divorced by twenty.

They fell in love young, married young, and divorced young.

Serena sighed heavily, before dropping the ring atop the clutter of other jewelry with a "ding". She missed Malcolm, her best friend, but not Malcolm, her husband. Amazing that they were one and the same.

She started to call her friend Monique Atkins and see what she had on her agenda for the night, but thought against it. Monique's weekend nights usually meant a short dress and a long night in some club. Serena had passed that phase in her life even if her friend hadn't.

Serena removed the beautiful wool boatneck sweater and wool skirt she had been wearing. A lazy night in front of the television, warmly snuggled beneath her comforter was just fine by her. Winter wasn't her favorite season and the crispness in the October air alluded to its onset. She finished undressing and slid her favorite fuzzy pink pajamas onto her sleek nude frame.

Serena absolutely loved being a beautician, but standing on her feet all day gave the small of her back and her feet major hell. Her dream was to open her own salon next year, so she was saving every bit of extra money she could to make that dream a reality. If she was going to work hard on her feet all day then she wanted to be working for herself.

Moving to her kitchen, Serena grabbed some left-over chicken chow mein from the fridge. As she warmed it in the microwave, she flipped through her mail. "Bills . . . bills . . . junk . . . bills," she said aloud, as she leafed through the stack of envelopes.

Serena threw a stack of junk mail into the trash. The phone rang and she crossed the tiled kitchen floor to grab her cordless. "Hello?"

"Serena Saint James?" a masculine voice asked.

Assuming it was one of those annoying telemarketers or a creditor, Serena snapped, "Yes?"

"How're you doing? This is Hamp. Hampton Tyler."

Serena didn't know why a chill raced through her body like quicksilver, but it did. Hampton "Hamp" Tyler was the Saint James' family attorney, or rather the attorney of Malcolm's grandmother, "Mama" Olivia Saint James. Over the years she had spoken to Mama James periodically, but hadn't been contacted by Hamp since the divorce.

Something was wrong.

"Serena, are you still there?"

"Yes, I'm sorry, Hamp. How you doing?" she said, her voice whisper soft.

"I wish I were calling you under better circumstances," he began.

Serena became nauseous with fear. Her knees weakened beneath her. *Oh no . . . Malcolm!*

"Olivia left very clear instructions that you were to be contacted upon her death."

Serena went still.

"Mama James is dead? Oh, my God," she sighed, her voice hollow as pain clutched terribly at her heart. The woman was an invincible force. A constant. Never had Serena pictured her in death.

Mama James had always been kind to her and the affection deepened when Serena and Malcolm began to date. No one could've been more pleased at their wedding, nor more upset because of their divorce. On how many occasions had she tried to talk Serena into giving their marriage another try?

And now Mama James was gone.

"What happened?" she asked, closing her eyes as pain washed over her in waves.

"She passed away in her sleep."

Serena nodded, unable to gather any more words.

"The funeral's this Thursday at Tabernacle Baptist Church at one o'clock and the will reading's Friday at my offices downtown."

Serena's pretty face became a mask of confusion as she held the phone with trembling hands. "No, no, I won't be at the will reading, Hamp," she asserted, as the tears gathered in her eyes.

"You have to be, Serena, you're mentioned in the will."

"I am?" she asked in surprise.

Hamp went on to give her directions to his office with clear instructions to be there by nine A.M. sharp.

"Hamp?" she asked, calling out his name before he could disconnect the line.

"Yes, Serena?"

"How's Malcolm?" she asked, surprising herself.

"We haven't been able to contact him at his place in New York. He's out of town. Something to do with a new documentary."

They ended the call after that.

So Malcolm's doing his documentaries. Whenever Mama James had tried to bring his name up during one of their sporadic conversations, Serena would politely change the subject until the older woman finally gave up trying.

Serena thought of her ex-husband and her chest

tightened. Funny, ten years after their divorce, and she hadn't laid eyes on the man since, but he still had the power to hurt her. They say time heals all wounds.

They were wrong.

Still, even though she could easily choke Malcolm she empathized with the grief he would feel at the news of Mama James' passing.

When Malcolm's mother died during his toddler years, his father was left to raise him alone, relying heavily on his own mother to help with his young son. Malcolm spent summers and all holidays with Mama James. The two had been very close. To him, she was the mother he never had.

Needing someone to talk to, Serena snatched up her cordless phone again and quickly dialed Monique's phone number. Her flamboyant friend picked up on the second ring.

"Hey girl."

"Hello, Ms. Serena Saint James, long time no hear from."

"Phone lines work both ways, Monique," Serena said, only somewhat playfully.

Monique was a little self-absorbed but Serena loved her to death.

"You'll never guess what all happened to me today," Serena began, leaving the kitchen to sprawl across her bed.

"You won the lottery."

"No."

"You met a celebrity."

Serena rolled her eyes heavenward because she knew if she let her, Monique could go on like that all night. "Monique," she snapped.

"Well, excuse the hell out of me."

"Anyway, first Zander decides to propose and then—"

Monique sucked air between her teeth. "That's the

Mama's Boy right. Shee-it, he got to get up off his mama first."

"Well, I turned him down."

"I'm surprised you're still dating him."

"You ain't the only one." Serena flopped over onto her back. "Anyway, do you remember Malcolm's grandmother Olivia Saint James?"

"Yeah."

At the mention of her name, Serena felt swamped with sadness. "She passed away," she said tenderly, closing her eyes at the ache she felt.

"Oh no," Monique moaned softly. "Wow, that's sad. She was so—wait . . . I got another call."

Serena wiped the tears from her eyes as she waited for Monique to click back over. She had so many emotions that she needed to get off her chest. Olivia's death. The will reading. Seeing Malcolm again. Zander's proposal. It was at moments like these that she yearned for Auntie. Her aunt and guardian would know the right thing to say and would offer her lap for Serena's head to rest in without a pause.

"Serena, that's Reebie, let me call you back."

Serena held the phone away from her face and looked at it with an agitated expression. "Enjoy the club," she said dryly, already knowing that's what the two of them were scheming up on.

"I'll get enough drink on for me and you."

Monique clicked back over without missing a beat.

Serena rolled on the bed and placed the cordless phone on the base. "Ain't nothing worse than a one-sided friendship," she mumbled, remembering just why she sometimes lost touch with her wild best friend.

She felt her stomach fill with nerves. Was it her curiosity over her part in Olivia's will or was it because in less than a week she'd be face to face with her ex again?

She honestly didn't know.

* * *

Malcolm Saint James flung the snifter of Crown Royal he'd been sipping into the fireplace. The addition of the alcohol immediately caused the flames to flare up in a red roar.

"Damn it!" he yelled, dropping his smooth bald head down into his hands as he sat on the chaise lounge.

Just three days ago he was wrapping up pre-production of one of his biggest projects to date: *Hip-Hop Domination*, a lengthy and detailed documentary on the widespread influences of hip-hop that was being funded by a consortium of the four largest urban record label owners in the industry. Today? Well, today he was going to see his beloved grandmother be buried in the cold, hard earth. He felt like a piece of himself would be in that casket with her.

This house, *her* house, was so ironically alive with her presence that he expected her to walk into the room at any moment, bringing the scent of White Diamonds perfume with her. She was gone forever. His life would never be the same.

The same drink he flung into the flames he craved with an intensity that scared him. He wanted to forget, but alcohol was a weakness to which he would never succumb. No, he had to be a man and face yet another major loss in his life.

Rising, he shoved his strong, massive hands into the pockets of his tailored slacks, moving around the room to study the multitude of photographs Mama James possessed. It was easy to see that he was the only grandchild. Most of the pictures were of him at various stages of life: his birth, his multitude of birthday parties, his graduation from high school, and his wedding.

Malcolm shook his head at the prominence Mama James gave the 8"x10"-framed wedding photograph of him and Serena. His grandmother had been a die-hard romantic who swore the childhood sweethearts should, could, and would be together again one day. She had stated that opinion on every given opportunity, whether big and bold: "You need to be with your wife," or sly: "I wonder if Serena's dating again."

Releasing a breath heavy with emotion, Malcolm let his eyes rest on Serena's face in the photo. She looked up at him with pure love and adoration. He remembered that very moment well. They had just been pronounced man and wife.

More like boy and child wife, he thought. They had only been eighteen, fresh out of high school, and eager to finally get into one another's pants. They graduated in June and were married in July.

Neither of their families had been overly pleased at the idea of their marriage, but when Malcolm and Serena threatened to run away and elope, Mama James had put her foot down. She called a meeting with Serena's aunt and her own son, Malcolm's father, and made her point quite clear: "They're in love and want to be married. Marriage is hard enough in the beginning without having to deal with angry parents to boot. Better to support them and give them guidance than send them off into this world alone. Now, I'm throwing a wedding. You in or you out?"

Just like that, the matter was resolved.

Serena and Malcolm grew up together and then grew apart, until all they shared were angry words. The last few months of their marriage they had been miserable in each other's company. To this day he wished they'd never wed. It was the biggest mistake he ever made in his life. He lost a friend and gained an ex-wife.

"It's time to head to the church, Malcolm. Your father's already waiting in the car."

Turning away from the past, Malcolm faced Hamp as the man continued walking into the den. "Thanks again for being such a good friend to Mama James."

"No problem, son. Olivia was a good friend and a very special woman," Hamp told him, sadness brimming in his eyes and his voice. "I still can't believe that she's gone."

"This house just won't be the same without her," Malcolm observed, looking around the den at his grandmother's prized possessions.

Mama James had not been a wealthy woman, but she had certainly been regal. She took pride in herself and the modest two-story English Tudor where she raised first her son, and then her grandson. Each piece of furniture, whether an inexpensive piece with wood veneers or a heavy antique piece from a secondhand store, was lovingly chosen and then cherished by her over the years. This house was the very essence of Olivia Saint James.

"We should be going," Hamp said, breaking into Malcolm's thoughts.

Malcolm nodded, solemn.

His life would never be the same.

The next morning Serena smoothed her hands over her pale peach three-quarter-length coat before entering the brick duplex that housed the downtown offices of Tyler Legal Services. She was so nervous that her hands shook as she opened the glass door.

What was her involvement in the reading of Olivia Saint James' will?

What would Malcolm think of her presence?

She wondered if he was still as angry at her as she was at him. Yes, ten years had not lessened the animosity she had for her ex-husband. She honestly didn't know if she could ever forgive him.

That didn't stop her from wanting to dress to the nines and show him that, like fine wine, she had only gotten better with time. Serena had absolutely no interest in a tearful reunion with her ex-husband, but she wouldn't mind him realizing just what he's missing.

Although a good thirty pounds heavier than the last time they'd seen each other, every bit of it had fallen onto the right places: fuller breasts, hips, and thighs, but a stomach as flat as a wall. Size twelve never looked so damn good. And it looked especially right in the curve-hugging suit she wore.

She certainly had been surprised at his own change of appearance when she caught sight of him at the funeral the day before. His physique was more toned, his handsome face more refined. His head was now clean shaven and it perfectly suited his keen features, emphasizing the smooth bronze of his skin and the mocha of his deep-set eyes.

Serena could never deny that Malcolm was a handsome man. The years had certainly been good to him, but they'd been just as good to her.

She doubted if he even knew she and Monique had been there. Her attendance hadn't been about Malcolm, she just wanted to pay her respects to Mama James. She could not care less if she ever laid eyes on Malcolm again. Unfortunately, she had no choice.

"Ms. Saint James?"

Serena smiled and nodded at the young, pretty receptionist sitting behind the front desk. "Yes."

"Mr. Tyler's waiting for you. Right this way."

Serena clutched her purse, trying desperately to fight off her nerves as she followed the other woman down a long corridor. *Chin up, Serena.* As she stepped though the door, her ebony eyes immediately scanned the occupants of the room.

Hamp sat behind an impressive mahogany desk.

Luther, Malcolm's father, sat in one of the chairs in front of the desk. Sitting on a leather sofa in front of the bay window was an older couple she didn't recognize. She didn't see Malcolm at all.

All eyes rested on her and Serena felt a fine sweat break out in the deep valley between her breasts. She smiled weakly in greeting. "Hello, everyone."

Hamp rose with a smile. "Come in, Serena. Come in."

"Serena?"

She whirled around at the sound of *his* voice and came face to face with Malcolm as he stepped from behind the open door. For one brief moment, as their eyes locked, she allowed herself to regret what could never be between them. But just for one second. Pain and anger at him consumed her like it was yesterday that he broke her heart and not ten years ago.

"Malcolm," was all she said with a stiff nod that spoke volumes.

"Serena," he countered, his voice filled with just as much anger and resentment.

The room became quiet enough to hear a straight pin hit carpet.

Hamp shook his balding head in dismay. As he watched the two turn away from each other like strangers, he definitely questioned the wisdom of Olivia's actions, and wondered what repercussions it would wrought.

"You have got to be kidding!"

Malcolm felt like Serena took the words right out of his mouth. Had Mama James lost her mind? Had Hamp for following through with her absurd request?

"Leave it to Ma to have her say even in death," Luther said, sounding amused.

Malcolm's eyes cut to his father and his suspicions were confirmed by the grin Luther wore. "I don't see what's so funny, Pops," he drawled.

Of course his father could laugh because he would receive his inheritance with no strings attached. As would Reverend Tisdale and his wife, Elizabeth, on behalf of his grandmother's church. Malcom was the only person in the will who had *stipulations* to meet first. Well, both Serena and he.

Malcolm turned from the bay window and glanced at Serena, who wore a pained expression.

It was *so* obvious what Mama James' intentions were. A last chance effort at reconciliation. The woman was playing matchmaker from the other side.

"Could you all leave us alone?" Malcolm stated more than asked, moving to pull the office door open.

"Couldn't say it any plainer than that, could he?" Sister Tisdale said with an amused smile, pulling her husband to his feet.

Serena rose as well.

"Stay, Serena," Malcolm ordered, before turning his attention to his father, whom he gave a long, hard, and meaningful stare.

"It was good seeing you again, Serena," Luther told his once daughter-in-law with a smile his son inherited. "Son, I'll be right outside if you need me."

"No, head on home. I'll stop by your place when I'm done here," Malcolm insisted, running his hand over his smooth bald head in obvious concern.

"Open your mind to the possibilities," Luther whispered to his son with a roguish wink, before taking his leave.

Serena faced Hamp. "Look, there's no need for me to remain. I am more than willing to forfeit—"

"Let's get this straight." Malcolm walked briskly past her to stand in front of the attorney's desk.

"I'll explain it to you both again," Hamp offered.

Serena held up her hands. "No need to explain for me. *I* understand, even if Einstein over there doesn't, and *I* want no part of it. Thanks, but no thanks."

"You haven't lucked up on a man yet to train you and that mouth of yours," Malcolm snapped, resting his eyes on hers.

"All my luck ran out July 7, 1992."

That was their wedding date.

"Yeah, mine too . . . until December 12, 1994," Malcolm countered.

The date their divorce was finalized.

They both turned to face the attorney, and stood side by side in front of his desk.

"Listen Malcolm, your grandmother left the house to you, *but* if you don't fulfill the terms of the will, total possession of the home and all of its contents— beside the ones bequeathed to your father, will revert to Tabernacle Baptist. They can then do with it as they please—except sell it back to you or any of Olivia's descendents. Serena, you won't receive the five thousand dollars Olivia left to you. For either of you to receive your inheritance you both must agree to take residence in the home for sixty days . . . together."

"This is ironclad?" Malcolm asked, ramming his hands into the pockets of his tailored slacks.

"Airtight," the attorney confirmed, looking from Malcolm to Serena.

"So I either live with her," he asked, jerking his thumb in Serena's direction. "Or I lose the family home?"

Hamp nodded again, steepling his long, slender fingers beneath his chin.

"Just wonderful," Malcolm frowned, slumping his tall, muscled frame into the seat his father had vacated.

"Hamp, it was really great seeing you again," Serena

told him, holding out her hand. "I'm sorry it couldn't have been under better circumstances."

"Malcolm, I'm really sorry that Mama James passed on. She meant a lot to me and I know that she meant even more to you."

Malcolm's sullen eyes rested on her and he was reminded of the fun days they shared as children. He begrudgingly nodded before looking away.

Hamp rose to take her hand. "I take it you don't agree to the terms."

"It would take more than five grand for me to agree to live under the same roof with this Neanderthal again. Good day, gentlemen."

With that said, Serena took her leave.

Interlude

Hello

1984

"Ya'll just move in?"

The little girl shifted her eyes away from the other girls she was watching play double-dutch, to the slender mocha-skinned boy sitting on his bike in front of her house. Before she answered him, she eyed first the basketball rammed between the handlebars of his bike and then the Polaroid instant camera hanging around his slender neck by a thin black strap. She figured him to be about eight. They were the same age. The big smile he wore was friendly enough. If there was anything the new kid in the neighborhood was looking for, it was a friend.

"We just moved in yesterday," she finally answered. "You live 'round here?"

"Yeah . . . no. Something like that."

Her small face filled with confusion and she frowned slightly as she eyed him. "Huh?"

"I live with my Pops in the Hallmark Apartments downtown, but my grandmother lives around the corner. I'm over her house a lot."

She wanted to ask, "Where's your Mom?", but she didn't. Her own parents died when she was three and she hated for anyone to ask why she lived with her aunt. She just nodded, squinting her almond-shaped eyes from the summer sun as she lazily picked at an old scab on one of her knobby knees.

"What's the camera for?" she asked him, filling the silence.

He shrugged. "I like taking pictures so my Pops bought this for me. I really wanted a video camera, but he misunderstood."

On impulse she stood and struck a pose, sucking in her cheeks and batting her long lashes, as she spread her slender arms wide. "Take my picture then, camera boy."

He laughed as he balanced his bike between his slender legs and lifted his camera to his face. "Say cheese," he urged her, still grinning.

"Cheddar," she murmured through her pursed lips as he took the picture.

She dashed down the stairs as he waved the instant photo to speed up its development. "Let me see."

"It's not ready yet," he told her.

She peered over his shoulder as the photo began to slowly appear before their eyes. They both began to laugh at the hysterical sight of her, an admitted tomboy in cut-off jeans, frizzy ponytail and baseball jersey, as she struck a model-like pose.

"You look hilarious," he said, with *too* much laughter.

She eyed him with attitude. He finally looked up and saw her expression. "Sorry," he mumbled, laughter still in his cocoa-brown eyes.

"I know you're sorry but do you apologize?" she countered quickly with sass.

"Huh?" he asked, confused.

But then they both burst out laughing.

"You wanna go down to the court in the park and watch them play ball?"

Her face broke into a smile. "Yeah."

"Put the ball on your porch and you can ride on my handlebars."

She raced to do as he suggested.

"What's your name anyway?" he asked, after she propped herself up onto the bike.

"Serena."

"I'm Malcolm. Malcolm Saint James," he said in return. "You ready?"

"Yup, let's roll, Saint James."

"It's just Malcolm," he offered. "Or Mal, but not Saint James."

"Uh-huh, sure."

Malcolm pushed off and then went rolling down the street.

Chapter 2

Two Weeks Later

"Okay, Meena. We're all done." Serena removed the cape from around her client's shoulders, before passing her a handheld mirror. She watched as Meena used the item to inspect the back of her ultra-short hairdo. The slender woman was one of Serena's regular weekly clients. She hoped Meena would follow her to her new salon—*when* she got it opened.

Or rather, *if* she got it opened.

Meena handed her seventy dollars plus a hefty tip. "See you next Friday, girl," she said over her shoulder, before sashaying out of the crowded salon with a final wave.

Serena grabbed her bottle of fruit punch, taking a large swig of it as she surveyed the large salon in which she rented a station. The place had once been stylish and had potential to be pleasantly presentable again. Currently though, it was sad and seriously neglected.

The silver, lavender, and blue décor was now faded and dull. The wallpaper was peeling and bubbling in random spots. The floor tile was chipped and some of its corners were stained with hair dye and other chemicals. The six hairdryers were mismatched and held together in places by duct tape.

That was just the tip of the iceberg of Serena's own list of complaints. Donald and Evelyn Warren, the owner/operators of Hair Happenings, just didn't see the need for costly improvements when their clients were still coming in strong. In fact, the couple had been offended by Serena's suggestions of their renovating.

So she'd just keep saving until she had enough to open her own salon. Even though she planned to start off with a small shop—maybe just three or four chairs—she planned on presenting a stylishly decorated salon with a professional staff and a drama-free environment. In time she planned to own and operate a full day spa offering every service a woman could imagine in one convenient and serene location. *I'll show 'em how it should be done.*

Serena was one of the more popular stylists in the salon and she made a good living, but she was in no way wealthy. Truth be told, she was up to her neck in monthly bills. It was hard to save the amount of money she would need to start her own business when she was catching hell paying the bills she already had. School loans, rent, car note, light bill, phone bill, cell phone bill, health insurance, food, clothes, and on and on and on.

Five thousand sure would help the cause.

No, it wasn't a lot of money, but she knew how precious that money had been to a hardworking woman like Mama James. Plus, it would be a nice sum to plump up her sad savings . . . or use as the security deposit for a lease on a small commercial property already set up as a salon.

Two months with Malcolm? She just couldn't do it! She wouldn't.

Monique walked into the salon just as another customer walked out. She was the best-dressed receptionist anyone had ever seen. The suit she wore was black in color but she livened it up with a patterned camisole and a bright brooch. Monique was fair skinned, slender, and wore her hair with an auburn infusion weave that Serena did for free. The last time was two months ago and Serena knew Monique was here to get it redone.

Serena's whole day was booked with appointments and she had two walk-ins already waiting. There was no way she could slide Monique in.

Serena started parting her next client's hair into four sections. "Hey, girl."

Monique leaned back against Serena's workstation. "Hey to you. You busy today?"

"Booked solid," Serena countered immediately

Monique pouted as she turned to study her reflection in the round mirror. "I wanted this out of my head but I guess it'll have to wait."

"I told you it's usually slow on Wednesdays," Serena said, as she used her gloved hand to smooth the relaxer into her client's new growth.

"Can't I just come by your house Monday?"

"When I open my shop, you know I'm gone charge you, right?"

Monique rolled her eyes heavenward. "Girl, please," she said dismissively. "You been talking 'bout opening that shop for years. So can you do my hair Monday?"

Serena swallowed a wave of irritation at Monique's nonchalance about her dreams. "I don't know yet."

The off-key chime on the front door sounded. Just as everyone else in the salon did, Serena and

Monique looked up to see who'd entered. Serena immediately froze at the sight of Malcolm.

Monique put her hand on her chest. "Look what the cat dragged in," she drawled, shifting her eyes to Serena.

Serena's heart double pumped and she detested that she was still so physically aware of the man. How betraying was her heart after what he did to her?

She watched as he questioned Evelyn, who was giving her own client a rod set in the front booth, before both Malcolm and Evelyn looked in her direction. Serena turned her head quickly, pretending she hadn't seen him as he headed in her direction.

"Damn it, he's a fine one," Serena heard her customer say.

Looking around, Serena noticed that almost all of the women—including her fellow beauticians and Monique—had their eyes glued to Malcolm. Frowning slightly, she shifted her gaze back to him.

"Wonder what he wants?" Monique whispered into Serena's ear.

"Probably about the will," Serena answered.

Monique frowned. "What will? Did Ms. Saint James have a will? You never said anything about a will."

"Sshh."

The camel-leather racing jacket Malcolm wore over a white tee—unfortunately known as a wifebeater—hung perfectly from his broad shoulders. The faded jeans hung low on his narrow hips as he swaggered with the same confidence she'd seen develop in him during their pre-teens.

"Excuse me," he said to Ree, who looked up at him with an appreciative look. "Monique."

"Malcolm," she returned, her tone just as short.

"Serena, I need to talk to you."

She *hated* the commanding tone of his voice and her face immediately showed it. "The days of you snapping your fingers and me jumping are over, Malcolm," she retorted, low enough for his ears only . . . or so she thought.

Monique jerked her head up to look at Malcolm.

"You never jumped before," he drawled, piercing her with those damn eyes as he hooked his thumbs into the back pockets of his jeans.

Monique's head swung to Serena.

"Then what made you think I would start today?" she countered, her eyes fixated on the perm she was smoothing on the new growth.

"Serena."

She looked up at him, using her wrist to push a loose strand of her shoulder-length auburn-dyed hair from her cinnamon face. "Leave me alone, Malcolm," she told him, wanting to say more but very aware of all eyes on them.

He looked around the shop. "I'll wait," he stated, moving with ease to sit in one of the dryer chairs.

Malcolm looked quite out of place, but it was clear that he wasn't moving until he was good and ready . . . or until she agreed to talk to him.

"Girl, looks like you got enough on your hands for one day," Monique said, sticking her purse under her arm. "Call me."

Monique threw Malcolm one last evil stare before she strutted out of the salon.

Exasperated, Serena shook her head. "Come on, let me wash you, Ree."

"Girl, is that your man?" the other woman asked as soon as Serena led her to the shampoo area in the rear of the salon.

"Ex-husband," Serena answered shortly, adjusting the temperature of the water before she positioned the chair to tilt backward.

Ree must have got the hint because all further attempts at conversation ended. Generally Serena wasn't ever rude to her clients, but Malcolm made her feel testy.

His presence had to be because of the will. He hadn't made any attempts to contact her since the divorce; so why now? Certainly *he* hadn't changed his mind?

As the water pressure suddenly changed to just better than a slow drip, Serena became disgusted. She *could* put that money to good use.

Still, they'd aggravate each other within one week, so there was no way they could survive two months—or sixty days, or one thousand four hundred and forty hours, or an infinite amount of minutes—in each other's presence. The littlest thing used to set them off.

Serena remembered one blow-up they had over fruit juice. Malcolm wanted some and Serena hadn't gone grocery shopping like she'd promised. He called her lazy and she told him he was petty and childish. It was on from there. That night he slept on the couch and they didn't speak to one another for the next three days.

How silly was that?

Major issues like adultery or physical abuse had never been their problem. It was the everyday living together, and not compromising, that had defeated the love, ruined the marriage, and ended their friendship. They just couldn't seem to get along in cohabitation. So why try now?

Particularly since she doubted she'd ever forgive him for his part in their marriage ending. How could she?

Serena released a heavy breath and wrapped a towel around Ree's damp head. "Sit in my chair," she told her, making sure to clean the excess water and suds from around the sink before she followed her client. She was annoyed—but not surprised—to see Malcolm sitting exactly where she left him.

Serena ignored him until she finished wrapping

Ree's hair with setting lotion. "Excuse me," she told Malcolm, coming to stand next to him. "I need this dryer."

He was leaning forward on his knees and he tilted his head back to look up at her. "Can we talk now?" he asked, his masculine voice deep and serious.

Just like the night he proposed.

Okay, Serena . . . don't even go there.

"If she won't talk to you, I will," one of the women in the salon called out, causing the rest of the patrons to laugh and high-five in agreement.

Serena didn't see anything funny. These women had no idea what she went through as her marriage crumbled around her. They had no clue as to how she fought to remain sane. They had no idea that was she still mad enough to claw his damn eyes out.

"I'm not leaving 'til you talk to me," he insisted, those eyes still locked on her.

She knew he meant it.

Serena reached behind him to turn on the dryer. Malcolm stood and Serena settled Ree in the chair. *Okay, Malcolm, you want some of me. Come and get it,* she thought spitefully. "We can talk in there," she told him with false sweetness.

Serena led him into the tiny and unorganized break room. As soon as she closed the door behind them, she said, "What the hell you want from me, Malcolm, huh?" she questioned him with all the anger she had and all the sistah-girl attitude she could muster as they stood toe to toe. "Why are you in my space . . . my . . . my life? Why are you here? What? What do you *want*?"

"My grandmother's house," he stated simply, looking directly down at her with those intense eyes.

"After what *you* did to *me* you think I care about what you want? Huh, you think I give a damn?" Her voice rose as the pain she thought she buried resurfaced like a geyser.

She wished she could put on a cool façade and pretend that she'd gotten over it all . . . but she couldn't.

"Don't do this, Serena," Malcolm commanded, looking away in what she took to be guilt.

She laughed bitterly as she turned her back on him. *Get it together, Serena. Don't even give him the pleasure of seeing your pain. Screw him.*

"That house meant a lot to my grandmother and it means just as much to me. I will not lose it, Serena."

She took a deep breath and faced him with a nonchalant look that made her proud. "And I will not be forced into a situation in which I am not comfortable."

A stand-off.

Malcolm pinched the bridge of his nose and then wiped his mouth with his hand. "Look, maybe I haven't approached this the right way."

Serena nodded and then began clapping—hard, slow, and deliberately sarcastic. "Finally, you've said *something* smart."

His eyes looked up to the ceiling before focusing back on her. "I had the will examined and it's airtight. Although I don't agree with my grandmother's actions, I don't want our family home to be lost because of it. That's just too much blame for me to carry on my shoulders alone."

"God forbid," she muttered sarcastically.

"Serena."

For one millisecond, as she heard the sincerity in his tone and saw it in his eyes, she was taken back to a time when they had been great lovers and best friends. That time had long since passed. "No."

"I'll add an additional twenty thousand," Malcolm countered smoothly, slipping his hands into the back pockets of his jeans.

He said it like twenty thousand dollars was nothing but pocket change; maybe to him it was.

"I see you're still doing hair. Haven't gotten your own
salon though. Twenty-five grand could go a long way."

Their eyes locked at the truth in his words.

"Truce?"

Silence reigned.

Her thoughts were a battle of his betrayal and her
own business. Which was greater to her? The past or
her future?

With reluctance she accepted his offer. "Truce."

One Week Later

"Do you think Serena will like her room, Malcolm?"

He paused to look up from the laptop, where he
was reviewing the shooting script for *Hip-Hop Domination*. He glanced over at his father, who sat on the
sofa watching television. "I don't see any reason why
she shouldn't. Your latest lady friend did a good job
of getting it ready."

Luther smiled at his son's reference to his fiancé.
"Her name's Elaine and we're getting married, son."

Malcolm shook his head, smirking as he focused his
piercing eyes back onto the computer screen. "You're
actually gonna make it down the aisle this time?"

Luther laughed good naturedly. "Okay, okay. I
know I've been down this road quite a few times—"

"Sixteen," Malcolm asserted with a laugh, as his
strong fingers skillfully worked the mouse. "Sixteen
times since I've been ten that you've been engaged.
And how many times did you actually get married?
That's right . . . zip."

Luther held up his hand. "Okay, okay. That's true,
but Elaine's different."

Malcolm snorted in derision. "We'll see."

"Serena sure has blossomed."

Malcolm tensed, knowing where the conversation was headed. "She looks the same to me," he said, deliberately sounding off-handed.

"A lie ain't nothing to tell."

His father was right, he was lying. When he first saw Serena at the funeral, he immediately noticed she put on a little weight and could definitely be considered more voluptuous than before. Gone was the slenderness of her late teens to be replaced by a softer, more appealing look in her early thirties. There was more of an air of confidence about her as well. She looked comfortable in her skin; and what beautiful skin it was. Being a divorcée seemed to suit her more than being his wife.

Her looks had changed, but not the attitude. Two months of Serena's explosive temper could—and probably would—drive him as insane as it had in the past. Just like her cleaning habits, or lack of them.

Serena had been a slob with a capital S. When it came to personal hygiene she had always been on point. In fact she used to love taking scented baths that lasted every bit of thirty minutes or more; but when she exited the bathroom it looked like a hurricane went through it with all the damp towels and discarded clothes on the floor.

Her sloppiness—and indifference about it—had led to many a heated argument between them. As had her inability to take the money he gave her to pay bills on time, not wanting to keep a job, and filling her days hanging out with her girlfriends.

Sadly, their marriage eventually thrust them apart instead of drawing them closer together. When they divorced he lost not only his wife but his best friend.

Malcolm wouldn't admit to anyone that he hadn't found a woman who could compete with the sexual enthusiasm he found in Serena. She was the absolute best lover he ever had. Her ardor in bed had been just as fiery as her temper. He honestly didn't know if her eyes blazed hotter with anger or passion.

His gut tightened thinking of some of the rather heated moments they had once shared.

As angry as she used to make him, months after their divorce he hated the thought of another man making love to her, and he certainly didn't want to risk running into her and her new man. That was the real reason he'd moved to New York.

No, sex had never been the problem; just every other aspect of the marriage.

What would the next sixty days hold? What was his grandmother hoping to accomplish? Surely she didn't think this would bring about a reconciliation between Serena and him?

Malcolm snorted in derision. He'd rather eat nails than remarry Serena and her big-time attitude. Great sex or not.

"Zander, I'm sorry, but we're at two different places in our lives. Since we've come to this crossroad, we must continue along on our different paths." Serena frowned at her reflection as she practiced just how she was going to break up with Zander.

"Zander, I think you're a wonderful man but we want different things out of life and I just want to . . ."

Serena released a breath. The last thing she wanted to do was hurt someone. She wanted to say the right thing to ease as much of his discomfort that she could.

"Oh, Zander's it's not you . . . it's me," she said with dramatic flare, wringing her hands in frustration.

"Okay, Serena, get it together, girl. He'll be here any minute," she said aloud to herself, rubbing her damp palms on her pants leg as she walked over to the open suitcase on her bed.

She was packing for her move into Olivia's house with Malcolm. *God, am I crazy?*

She'd never want to go back to the place she was in as her marriage collapsed around her. Losing Malcolm had been one of the hardest events of her life.

Serena's eyes shifted to her open closet. With slow, measured steps she walked to her closet and reached up to the disheveled top shelf to extract a large floral box—a box she hadn't dared to look in for years. She sat down on the floor, crossing her legs Indian style as she slowly pulled off the lid to her past with Malcolm.

Inside was every bit of memorabilia from their years together. Serena searched through the layers. Dried roses and cards from special holidays and anniversaries. Love letters. Concert ticket stubs. Photos. Dozens and dozens of photos. Serena smiled at the Polaroid picture Malcolm took of her the first day they met. *Look at me making a silly face,* she thought. *I was just happy somebody wanted to be my friend.*

"And he was a good friend," she said aloud huskily, tears forming in her eyes. These photos reminded her of the awesome friendship she and Malcolm shared as kids. As friends, Malcolm had never intentionally hurt her feelings. As friends, Malcolm had been the one she ran to to work out her problems. As friends, Malcolm had always put her needs first. If only they hadn't crossed that line . . .

Ding-dong.

Zander.

She took a deep, steadying breath as she wiped away the tears and then scooped up all her memories and shoved them back in the box.

Ding-dong.

"Coming," she yelled out, rising from the floor to sit the box back in the closet.

Serena practiced her speech as she walked to the door, but all of the words failed to resurface once she had Zander sitting on the sofa beside her.

"I thought you wanted to tell me something." Zander said after long moments of silence.

Serena locked her eyes with his. "I do. I . . . I . . . just don't know how to say it."

Zander's face became tight with understanding. He nodded his head several times, released a short breath, and looked up to the ceiling. "What? Is this the time for the great 'It's not you, it's me' speech?" he asked, removing his glasses to clean in a decidedly agitated gesture.

Did he read my mind? Serena wondered as she flushed with embarrassment. *Okay, plan B.*

"Zander, I'm sorry, but we're at two different places in our lives. Since we've come to this crossroad, we must continue along our different paths," Serena said softly, hating the melodramatic words as soon as she said them. *Lord, I sound like Scarlet O'Hara. I wouldn't blame him if he didn't give a damn.*

Zander slid his glasses back onto his face. "If this is about getting married, I'm willing to wait."

"Zander, you are a good man and you will make some woman a really good husband, but I have no intention of getting married again." Serena reached over and grasped his hand. "So I guess this is the 'It's not you, it's me' speech."

Zander stood and walked around Serena's living room. He walked past the hall and then stopped. He took two steps backward and looked directly into Serena's bedroom. "Going somewhere?" he asked, turning his head to look at her.

Serena nodded. *Oh Lord, here we go.* "I've decided to accept the terms of Olivia's will."

Zander's body tensed and he dropped his head. "Is this why you won't marry me?"

Serena felt irritated by the whine in his voice, but she was sympathetic to his feelings. "No, that's not the reason at all and you know it."

"No, Serena, I don't know a *damn* thing. I didn't know you never wanted to get married again. I didn't know you were going to break up with me and turn down my proposal. And I damn sure didn't know that you're moving in with your ex."

"Zander—"

"Serena, I am totally against this. This just isn't appropriate," he insisted. "What will my mother think?"

A wave of irritation filled her, nipping at her neck like gnats. "I really don't give two shakes of a donkey's ass what *your* momma does or doesn't think about what I do with *my* life."

Okay, bringing up his mama struck a nerve.

Zander looked insulted. "You're being unreasonable."

"No, I'm not."

"You seem pretty damn eager to get back into a living situation with your ex."

"No, I'm eager to open my own salon and twenty-five grand is going to help get it done."

"To what end are you willing to go to open this . . . this *little* salon."

Serena froze, turning around slowly to stare at him with a less-than-pleased look on her pretty face. "Excuse me?"

"You heard me," he asserted, even though there was a hesitation in his eyes that she could see through his glasses.

"I don't appreciate you insinuating that I will do anything, including sell myself, to open my *little* salon." Serena pierced him with her eyes. "Zander, this isn't about us. It's about me. I'm going to get this money and then I'm going to open my salon."

"I wonder what else he has to offer that you'll take."

Serena literally screamed out in frustration at his shortsightedness and flung her hands up in the air. With that said, Serena walked to the front door and opened it wide.

He stared at her in disbelief for several awkward seconds before he slowly walked up to her. "If you insist . . . " he let the words drift off before he held out his hand.

"Brotha, you ain't said nothing but a word." Serena strode so quickly into her bedroom that she could have made a trail of fire between her heels, returning just as quickly with the burdensome engagement ring in her hand. Staring him straight in the eye, she dropped it into his awaiting palm.

His expression became astonished. "Mama said you had shifty eyes."

Serena used a hand to guide him out the door. "You know Zander, if your mama would learn to give your grown behind milk from a cup and get you off her titty, she might find some business of her own to get up in. So, you and your *ma-ma* have a nice life . . . together. See ya!"

With that said Serena slammed the door in his face with too much pleasure. She felt like a school teacher who had just sent an unruly student to the principal's office—relieved.

Zander wanted too much too soon. He was a good man overall and he deserved a woman who wanted the whole "happily ever after" package: a husband, two kids, a clingy mother-in-law, white picket fence, and a dog named Scooby. It all just wasn't for her. She'd been there, done that, and failed miserably.

* * *

Mama James' house was on 16th Avenue in Newark, New Jersey. The modest home was a source of pride and joy for her and Papa James when they first purchased it over fifty years ago. He had worked as a custodian for the school district and she had been a day maid for a prominent family in Maplewood. When Olivia and Elvin moved into the three-bedroom home with their one son, they had plans of having a large family to fill the rooms with lots of laughter and love. No other children ever followed Luther, but there had been plenty of the love and laughter that they desired.

When Elvin passed away at the young age of forty from a stroke, Mama James quickly stepped up as the matriarch of the small family. She saved the insurance money she received after her husband's passing and continued to work, paying the mortgage and making sure Luther never lacked for the essentials.

Serena turned her car into the driveway behind a silver Cadillac Escalade that she assumed was Malcolm's. She tooted her horn twice before she climbed out of the vehicle. As she began to pull one of her suitcases and carryall from the trunk, Malcolm stepped out of the front door.

For one second, Serena felt like they were still married and she was just retuning home after running errands. This moment reminded her so much of the life she had wanted to have with Malcolm: their own home, him awaiting her arrival, their lives happy.

She stood on the sidewalk and looked up at the modest but still impressive house. "Olivia, what were you thinking?" she asked softly, shifting her eyes up to the clear, blue sky.

Chapter 3

"How much did you pack, Serena? It's just two months, or don't you plan on washing clothes?"

And *poof*, just like that, he opened his big mouth and the moment passed with the wind. Serena sucked air between her teeth, more than agitated, and ignored him as she pulled another of her suitcases from the trunk and headed for the house.

As soon as she hit the door the faint scent of White Diamonds perfume, Mama James' favorite, assailed her. A deep sadness settled about her shoulders. She hadn't been in this house for years. Without Mama James it just didn't feel the same.

"It seems like she'll walk out the den at any moment, doesn't it?"

Malcolm's voice was so close that it startled Serena a bit. She turned her head to look at him over her shoulder. "I'm really sorry that she's gone, Malcolm," she told him softly, her voice sincere.

Their eyes locked briefly before he cleared his throat and nodded his head, breaking the moment. "Thanks . . . um, your room is upstairs. Follow me."

Malcolm walked past her to jog up the stairs with

her other two suitcases held easily in his strong grasp. Serena followed at a slower pace, eventually coming to the only room on the second floor where the door was open wide. It was obviously freshly aired with crisp, fresh linens. .

"This room hasn't been used in years. Elaine got it ready for you," he said, setting the luggage on the neatly made bed.

"Elaine?" Serena asked, hating that she immediately envisioned this faceless woman as Malcolm's lover.

His eyes darted to her knowingly. "Pop's latest fiancé."

Serena laughed lightly. "Is he *still* doing that? How many women has he proposed to over the years?"

Malcolm actually smiled, his strong white teeth brilliant against the bronze tint of his smooth skin. "Sixteen. I'll admit it, I'm actually keeping count."

They became silent and then the silence became awkward.

"The bathroom's down the hall to the right and the kitchen is—"

Serena unzipped the first large suitcase and then turned to face him. "Malcolm we lived here, in this very room as a matter of fact, when we first got married. I think I'll remember where everything is," she said delicately. "In fact, there are just some things I'll never forget."

The bitterness crept back into her tone. Their cordialities were fine but she had not forgotten or forgiven the pain this man put her through.

He rested those piercing cinnamon eyes on her. "We need to talk, Serena."

She laughed harshly. "You didn't feel like talking all those years ago, so, please, don't feel like it now."

Serena forced herself to turn away from him, instead focusing her attention on scooping all of her undergarments into one arm. She used her free hand to pull open the top drawer of the mahogany dresser against the far wall. "I'm not here to make nice and pretend like shit didn't go down foul as hell between us, Malcolm," she told him, as she unceremoniously dropped the pile into the drawer and then used her curvaceous hip to close it.

Malcolm raised a brow. "We're both to blame for our break up," he said stoically.

Serena looked back at him, a pile of sweaters now in her hands. "Say what?" she asked, instantly annoyed.

"Nothing," he said huskily but sharply. "I have some errands to run, just help yourself to whatever's in the fridge."

"I'm here for my twenty-five grand—and that's it." Her voice was cold, even as hot waves of pain filled her chest and she fought back a desire to crumble with weakness.

He left the room.

Serena eventually heard his feet hitting the floor as he jogged down the stairs. "This was a mistake," she whispered aloud, as she sunk down onto the bed and let her head fall into her hands. "What have I done?"

Regret at her decision consumed her. Seeing Malcolm was more than she could handle. What made her think she could survive living with him? *Am I crazy?*

Malcolm had already given Hamp a cashier's check for twenty thousand dollars. In sixty days she would earn that check plus the five thousand bequeathed to her from Mama James. But what was she losing in the process? Self-respect? Her dignity? Her soul?

She swore she never wanted to lay eyes on Malcolm again, yet, here she was.

"Serena!"

She flinched. *What the hell does he want?*

"What?" she yelled back and then felt childish. She composed herself and then left the room and looked down to the foyer to find Malcolm and Hamp standing there.

"Hey, Hamp, how are you?"

The older gentleman looked up a her with a friendly and open smile. "I'm fine, I'm fine. Just doing my check."

Serena cocked a brow in confusion. "Your check?"

"I will be dropping by sporadically, and without warning, to ensure that you two are living up to your agreement to stay here. Just another of Olivia's stipulations."

Serena's eyes shifted to her ex before shifting back to Hamp. "You're kidding, right?"

Hamp didn't look any more pleased about the fact than Serena or Malcolm. "I could only wish. Olivia's motto was 'What you don't see for yourself, don't believe.'"

Serena smiled at the older woman's craftiness. "I've heard her dole out that piece of advice on many occasions. Well, I'll be damned. 'Scuse my language," she said immediately .

"Quite all right."

Malcolm pinched the bridge of his nose. "What if I have to go out of town for business?"

Hamp looked uncomfortable. "Not for the next two months—"

"That's ridiculous," Serena and Malcolm exclaimed in unison.

"My hands are tied."

"*His* hands are tied?" Serena muttered, feeling total annoyance.

"We can hear you, Serena," Malcolm called up to her dryly.

If looks could kill, Malcolm would have dropped on the spot.

"I'm gonna head on to church," Hamp said, turning to open the door. "See you both soon."

And he was gone.

"Must you always be rude?" Malcolm asked.

"Go to hell," she drawled with a suck of her teeth, before turning to enter her bedroom.

Serena headed straight for the bed. She picked up the remote, and turned on the television. She was ready to zone out for the rest of the day.

Malcolm did a double take when he entered the house through the kitchen. In fact he turned around, left the spacious room, and reentered it. "What the—"

The once neat and orderly kitchen now looked like a tornado had swept through it. A tornado named Serena. Sugar and coffee grains were all over the countertop. Coffee stains had congealed to the tile. The cabinet doors and drawers were ajar. The remnants of a half-eaten sandwich sat on a plate on the island, along with an open bag of potato chips just waiting to go stale. Something unidentified crunched beneath his feet when he walked across the room.

All these years later and the woman was still a slob.

Holding the bag of filming supplies he purchased, Malcolm headed out of the kitchen and up the stairs towards her room.

Reaching for her fluffy terry cloth towel, Serena laid it on the foot of the bed before she began to pull her baby tee over her head. Letting it fall to the floor, she reached up behind her to unclasp her red lacy brassiere, more than happy to let her grapefruit-sized breasts free. She began to work her jeans down her hips.

Her bedroom door flew open.

"What the hell?" Serena gasped, looking up to find Malcolm standing in the doorway.

His eyes dropped. Serena's hands raised. She covered each of her pendulous breasts as she eyed Malcolm angrily.

"Oh damn," he swore, immediately turning his back to her.

Serena reached for her shirt, pulling it over her head quickly. "Ever heard of knocking?" she snapped, as she jerked her arms through the sleeves and then pulled her jeans back up over her shapely hips.

Malcolm laughed shortly and mockingly, his broad back still to her. "It's not like I haven't ever seen what you have before," he drawled.

"Yeah, but your 'cop a free look when you want to card' has definitely been revoked," Serena told him with pleasure.

"Are you dressed now, Mother Theresa?" he asked, already beginning to turn his head to look over his shoulder towards her.

Serena opened her mouth to answer, but changed her mind.

"I'd advise you to grab a shirt and pull it on before I count to three."

"Bully," she whispered spitefully, thinking she was loud enough for just her own ears.

Malcolm turned, his eyes momentarily falling to her discarded lacy bra on the floor, before he looked up to meet her turbulent eyes. "Call me whatever names you want, Serena. You can be as big a slob as you want at your house, but we're living in a dump-free zone here."

Serena looked at him like he was a piece of gum stuck to the bottom of her shoe. "You couldn't boss me while we were married and you damn sure ain't gonna do it now."

Malcolm's shoulders heaved with his anger at her thoughtlessness. "For once you're right because I damn sure didn't want my wife up in the club with her friends."

"I was eighteen!"

"You . . . were . . . married!" he shouted back.

"I made mistakes but I never deserved what you did to me . . . and you know it," she countered with conviction.

Malcolm felt flooded with guilt. "Serena, I was wrong for—"

"No, no, no . . . no." She held up a hand, ready for the drama to cease.

His eyes pierced into her. "If you won't talk about it like adults, I'll just leave."

"Well, we both know you always do whatever you want to, now don't we?" she asked, her voice shaky with emotion as she alluded to their past.

He looked like he wanted to say something but changed his mind. "Sorry I barged into your room."

"I know you're sorry but do you apologize?" she threw back at him flippantly.

"Grow up, Serena," he mumbled, before turning to leave.

Childishly she stuck out her tongue.

The door slammed and he was gone.

Even though he had been a young husband, Malcolm had been so controlling and dominating to Serena. That completely clashed with the independence she'd cherished even at a young age.

Do this, Serena. Don't do that, Serena. Where are you going? Where have you been? Why? When? What? Who? How?

Aaahhh!

They knew each other for ten years before they said their I-dos and then it was like they'd never known each other at all. Okay, she was willing to admit that her Auntie and Luther had been right about them being entirely too young to get married. Only Mama

James had faith in them and stood up for them, and in the end they proved her wrong.

Serena was heading out of the bedroom to tackle the kitchen before she bathed, when her cell phone rang from her purse. She backtracked her steps and retrieved the phone. Zander's mother's phone number was displayed on her Caller ID. Switching the call to voice mail, she dropped it back in her purse.

The next morning Serena rose at seven, grabbed her toiletry kit, and padded barefoot toward the bathroom across the hall from her bedroom. As she neared the master bedroom where Malcolm was sleeping, she gave in to her curiosity about whether he came back to the house at all the night before. She justified her curiosity by concern over Hamp stopping by for a check and discovering that Malcolm fudged on the agreement.

Standing by his room, Serena leaned in close and placed her ear to the door. She tensed and leaned in closer when she heard a thump, clutching her toiletry kit to her chest. Suddenly her support disappeared and she fell sideways into the room, landing on the floor with a thud.

"Mornin' Serena," Malcolm drawled.

Expelling a heavy, audible breath, Serena felt swamped with embarrassment and allowed herself to stay pressed against the cool wood of the floor as she fought to regain what little composure she could.

When she dared to open her eyes, her line of vision was filled with Malcolm's bare, size-twelve feet and the hem of his pajama pants. *See Serena, curiosity did kill the cat,* she told herself as she rose to her feet with what little dignity she had left.

"Can I help you?" Malcolm asked mockingly, laughter in his deep set eyes.

Serena fixed her face into a picture of innocence and shrugged. "No," she said lightly, before turning to walk into the bathroom with her head held high.

As she gave herself a facial in the oval mirror over the pedestal sink, Serena tried hard to put the embarrassing scene behind her. She had more important things to worry about. Today she was a woman on a mission because she was going to start getting the necessary details to complete her business plan. And step one was finding a commercial property available for leasing that was within her budget. She wasn't stupid and knew that with her small amount of start-up capital, her best route would be acquiring a space that already served as a hair salon.

Monday was the only weekday she had off and she planned to use every available minute of it to get all her ducks in a row. Soon she would have an extra twenty-five thousand dollars in her bank account and she wanted to use that money so that she could be open for business at least three months later. Plain and simple.

Grabbing her loofah and body wash, Serena decided on a quick shower over her usual bath. It seemed she had just stepped under the steaming spray when she heard Malcolm knocking heavily on the door.

"Serena! I need the bathroom."

Even with the water running and the door being closed tightly, Serena heard Malcolm clearly. Rolling her eyes heavenward, she finished her shower and rinsed off the last of the citrus scented suds from her body with regret. Pulling back the cotton shower curtain and plastic liner, she reached for her towel, drying off before she wrapped the plush terry cloth around her body.

When they were married Malcolm had always complained about how much time she spent in the bathroom. Back then he would just get into the shower with her—which usually led to sex, or he'd use the facilities and leave.

Those days of intimacy definitely were over.

Serena gathered her items back into her kit and bundled her nightclothes under her arm. She'd forgotten to grab her robe, but *c'est la vie.* Besides, she knew there was no way Malcolm would be standing outside the door.

"I see you're still a bathroom hog. Hope you left me some hot water."

Serena nearly ran into him as she attempted to step out of the bathroom and had to halt in her tracks to avoid colliding with his body. "Male chauvinist pig," she muttered darkly, brushing past him to pad barefoot to her bedroom.

Thirty minutes later, dressed in a pair of jeans, a white turtleneck, and ankle boots, Serena grabbed her coat, wallet, and keys, and headed down the stairs and out of the front door. Malcolm was already loading boxes into the back of his massive SUV. He didn't speak to her, so she didn't bother with niceties either. Climbing into the driver's seat of her Honda Accord, she attempted to crank it three times and failed. Grimacing, she hit the steering wheel with her fist. She just put five hundred dollars into repairing the engine and now this.

"Something wrong?"

Serena looked up and saw Malcolm standing beside the driver's side door. "My car won't crank."

"Lift your hood," he told her with impatience.

Serena stuck her head out of the window. "Don't bother," she snapped, irritated that he made her feel like a nuisance.

Malcolm stared at her long and hard through the windshield before he came around the car, stuck his hand through the open window, and pulled the latch to release the hood.

Serena scrambled out of the car and came to stand beside him as he leaned under the hood. "I *said* don't bother," she reiterated.

"You probably need an alternator," he told her, completely ignoring her protests.

"A what?" she asked, peering down at all of the mechanics of her vehicle like she really knew what she was looking at.

"You got AAA or something? You're gonna need a tow," he told her, turning his head to look up at her.

"But I need my car *today*," she told him with emphasis on the last word. Serena stomped her foot in frustration and raised her fists to the sky, saying, "Damn . . . damn . . . damn!"

"I hear you, Florida Evans," he said dryly, speaking of the infamous scene played out by Esther Rolle on the seventies sitcom *Good Times*.

Malcolm lowered the hood. "I know a good mechanic in the area."

Serena shook her head. "No, it's my problem. I'll handle it. It just throws a kick in my plans for today."

Malcolm stared at Serena, his expression mildly surprised.

"What?" she asked as he continued to look at her.

"Nothing," he answered abruptly. "Listen I can drop you wherever you have to go. I was just on my way to run some errands."

Again Serena shook her head. "The last thing I want is *your* help, trust me."

"Still cutting your nose off to spite your face."

"Still a control freak," she countered.

"Why you so childish?" Malcolm grimaced as he looked down at her.

"Why you in my face?"

They squared off, standing nearly toe to toe, and

although animosity simmered between them like a quiet storm there was chemistry brewing as well.

Suddenly they both stepped back from each other.

Serena turned and headed up the sidewalk to the house, her mind busy working on getting her car to the mechanic. "I can, and will, handle this myself, Malcolm. I'm not an incompetent lady in distress, trust me."

"That's new," he chuckled from behind her.

Interlude

First Kiss

1989

"Hey, Mal."

Both Serena and Malcolm looked up from her bike that they were repairing in front of his grandmother's house. Three little mini divas stood there, stylishly girly in their Guess jean skirts and tank tops, with lip gloss tinting their lips and the summer sun bouncing off their ebony curls.

So unlike Serena.

Defiant, she pulled her New York Knicks cap down lower over her eyes and ignored them, hoping Malcolm would do the same.

Her best friend of five years was fast becoming fonder of cute little girls with ponytails and curls than bicycles, video games, basketball, *and* his tomboy best friend. When Malcolm rose to walk over to them, Serena looked out the corner of her eye in their direction.

As he socialized, she finished repairing the tire alone. Serena felt her anger rise. With every giggle from the girls, every bit of bravado from Malcolm as he showed off for his personal cheering squad, and every moment he left her to finish the task alone, Serena got even more ticked off.

"Bump him," she muttered to herself, as she quickly worked to inflate the tire.

Serena turned the bike back upright and hopped onto it. Not even looking back, she rode away like the very devil was on her heels. Her pedaling quickened when she heard Malcolm yelling her name. She didn't stop until she turned the corner and reached home.

Malcolm was determined to find out what was wrong with Serena. She had refused to come back outside all day and wouldn't even come to the phone when he called her.

"Girls," he muttered darkly, more than disgusted because Serena was acting like a typical female— something she usually didn't do.

She could run faster than all the boys on the block, including him, and she won all the free-throw contests easily. He could talk to her about anything and everything. They kept each other's secrets and fought each other's battles. Everyone knew that when you saw Malcolm you saw Serena, especially during the summers.

Except today.

Malcolm kept racking his brain to figure out what ticked her off and he continued to draw a blank. Not that it took much to make her mad with *her* temper. Still, he had to know. It was killing him not knowing.

Flinging back the covers, Malcolm rose from the twin bed in his room at Mama James'. He quickly pulled shorts over his boxers and grabbed a T-shirt as he slid his feet into his athletic sandals. As he left the bedroom, he glanced at the digital clock on his nightstand. It read 11:35 PM.

It didn't matter. He was determined to talk to Serena tonight.

Ping!
Serena snorted in her sleep before flopping onto her stomach in the middle of her full-sized bed.
Ping!
Jolted from sleep by the sudden noise, she lifted her head off the pillow as her eyes popped wide open. "Huh? What?"
Ping! Pang!
Serena scrambled from her bed, cloaked by darkness, and moved toward the window. Still rubbing the sleep from her eyes, she looked down to see Malcolm searching for another pebble to throw up at her second-floor bedroom window. She used her strong, slender arms to yank it up. A pebble hit her shoulder and she bit her bottom lip to keep from yelling out in pain. The last thing she needed was for Auntie to wake up and find Malcolm in her backyard.

Still rubbing her bruised shoulder, Serena left her bedroom. She peeped in Auntie's room to make sure she was still sleeping soundly. Assured that she was by a deep bearlike snore, Serena crept out the backdoor and descended the stairs. When she opened the heavy metal back door, Malcolm was just about to throw another pebble.

"Throw it and I'll snap your fingers off, Saint James," she told him, walking up to where he stood in the circle of light created by the fixture on the corner of the three-family house.

Malcolm turned toward her and his face filled with surprise. He seemed to be at a loss for words.

Serena made a face as he continued to stare at her like she had two heads and one eye. "What? What is it? Do I have sum'n hangin' from my nose?" she asked.

Malcolm looked down at the sandals on his feet. "Your hair's loose."

Serena immediately removed the scrunchee from her slender wrist and pulled her mass of frizzy curls back into a tight ponytail. "I know it's not as prissy as your little groupies, but you don't have to gawk at me."

He looked at her, his face now confused.

Serena placed a hand to her just developing chest and tilted her head to the side, comically batting her lashes. "Oh Malcolm, I just love the way you play basketball. Will you take my picture, Malsey Walsey? Can I model for you, Malcolm the Great? Can I smell your farts and lick your big ole funky feet!"

He watched as Serena made a face and then stuck her finger in her mouth, imitating throwing up. He smiled.

"All those prissy missies are stuck-up and phony, but you wouldn't notice that with all the stars in your eyes." Serena crossed her arms over her chest, glaring at her best friend.

"I notice a lot of things, Serena," he told her seriously, moving his already six-foot frame a step closer to her.

"Well good for you, Sherlock," she said sarcastically.

"I notice that you always smell like strawberries, and that you hum when you're doing your homework, and you bite your bottom lip when you're shooting free throws. And I noticed that you're growing in places you weren't growing before," Malcolm finished, his eyes dropping briefly to her chest before rising again.

For that, Serena punched him on the arm, feeling embarrassed.

"I just noticed that you're even prettier with your hair out," he told her softly and shyly, his eyes shifting from hers.

Serena was glad for her deep amber skin tone as

she felt her skin flush with warmth under his awkward praise. "*Whatever*, Saint James."

"You're the prettiest girl on the whole block, Serena," he added earnestly.

Serena knew when she started having the odd dreams about kissing Malcolm, that her feelings for him had moved beyond the brotherly stage. Now as he stood before her, fidgeting under her direct gaze, Serena knew that his feelings for her had changed as well. That pleased her infinitely.

He reached up and pulled the scrunchee from her hair, freeing her mass of frizzy curls. Serena's heart burst with joy and the tender strains of first love.

"Wanna kiss?" he asked awkwardly, as his fingers played lightly in her hair.

"'Bout time you asked, nimrod," she answered him softly with a smile, just as his head lowered to hers.

His lips touched lightly down upon hers.

It was soft and sweet. Perfect. Just the way she dreamed.

Their bodies stood a foot apart and their hands were at their sides as their lips remained locked, yet Serena never felt closer to anyone.

"Will you be my girl, Serena?" he asked softly against her lips, looking down into her eyes.

She nodded.

"Not mad at me anymore?" he asked, teasing.

"Nope."

He kissed her again quickly. "I better get back before Mama James finds out I'm gone. See you tomorrow, girlfriend."

"Okay, boyfriend," she answered with a goofy grin, as he turned and walked out of the yard, his tall figure disappearing into the darkness.

That night as Serena lay awake in her bed, she couldn't wait to see Malcolm again *or* to ask Auntie to press her hair so that she could wear it loose.

Chapter 4

The first two weeks at the house were uneventful. Serena and Malcolm barely spoke or acknowledged one another, acting more like strangers than two people who shared nearly all of the first twenty years of their lives together.

Luther said as much when he dropped by the house Saturday afternoon. "I guess Mama's plenty pissed up there in heaven," he noted, taking a seat next to his son in the den.

Malcolm felt his father's eyes shift to him and he knew where the conversation was headed. He played clueless. "Why's that?"

"The coldness between my daughter-in-law and you—"

"*Ex*-daughter-in-law," Malcolm interrupted with emphasis, shooting his father a meaningful stare.

"Yeah, whatever. Listen, the air between ya'll is frigid enough to chill the Antarctic," Luther continued, undeterred. "Not exactly the warm reunion Mama plotted and schemed to achieve."

Malcolm was actually proud of that. He meant to keep his distance from his fiery ex-wife. He was going to prove that he could—and would—live under the same roof with her without giving in to this romantic reunion everyone swore was inevitable.

He'd show them.

"Then again ya'll have way over a month and a half to go. Who knows . . . anything could happen." Luther crossed his ankle over his knee, swiping away a piece of lint from his pants.

"Trust me, anything *won't* happen."

"Son, if you took off those blinders I think you'll see that little Serena has grown into a confident, self-assured, and independent woman."

Malcolm pretended to ignore his father, but truth be told he *had* noticed. For as long as he could remember, Serena had always needed him. She used to always run to him to solve her problems. Always. He had become accustomed to taking care of Serena, but he saw the change in her. Just thirty minutes after her car broke down, she had it towed and scheduled for repair. Two days later, she was on the road again and not once did she ask for his assistance.

And he had to admit that he was surprised to find that she spent her nights holed up in her bedroom watching television or reading. Visions of loud-mouthed girlfriends—like Monique, God forbid, sporadically dropping over with bottles of Alizé and margarita mix hadn't emerged. On her days off he would see her poring over the classified section for real estate or on the phone pricing supplies. It appeared that his wife—the woman who was awful at working, cleaning, and paying bills was gone. Still, he wasn't naive, it was way too early to judge.

And well . . . there were other changes as well.

Her body had softened and developed into that of a sultry and voluptuous woman. A woman molded and developed for the strong hold, caress and loving of a man. Breasts ample enough to sate a brotha's appetite. A deeply curved waist made to be grasped. Thighs thick enough to surround her man as she drew his hardness into her sugar walls with ease.

Sugar walls that he could remember kissing, stroking, and probing all too well.

He would admit to no one that ever since he walked in on Serena getting undressed that he was distracted with the constant memories of just how beautiful her body was. Last night he even dreamed of burying his face in the deep valley between her breasts as his hands got lost between her strong and shapely thighs.

Her walking out of the bathroom in the morning, clad only in a damp and clinging towel that stopped midthigh above long shapely legs, had him feeling amorous. And then to walk in the bathroom and be surrounded by her citrus scent, or standing in the shower where she had just stood naked and wet, was getting to be pure torture.

Uh-oh.

So he was even more determined to keep the distance between them. He was just as aloof and cold as she.

Ding-dong.

Luther rose to look out the window. "Who's this cat?" Luther asked, his tone curious as he eyed the tall slender man standing at the front door.

Malcolm shrugged, reaching for his super-sized glass of fruit punch. "Probably just a Jehovah's Witness," he answered dryly, taking a huge sip of the sweet liquid before he rose to walk over and open the door.

Luther mumbled something under his breath.

"Can I help you?" Malcolm asked, not recognizing the man.

"Only if you're Malcolm Saint James."

Malcolm became alert and felt his father walk up

behind him. "And you are?" he asked coolly, his eyes locked on the man.

"Zander Madison."

Malcolm stood waiting for the rest of the introductions. When none was forthcoming, he said, "Are you selling something? What?"

"I'm Serena's fiancé," Zander countered with emphasis.

Malcolm was surprised, but he didn't reveal that fact. "Really? Serena hadn't mentioned you."

Zander definitely didn't have a poker face. His eyes widened just before his light complexion reddened with some emotion, be it anger or embarrassment. "What kind of man uses some bogus will to get a woman?" he asked stiffly.

"What kind of man allows his fiancée to move in with another man?" Malcolm countered, shooting the man a disparaging look.

"Stay the hell away from Serena," Zander shouted in anger.

Malcolm first smiled and then laughed deep, rich, full and completely mocking. "Now that will be hard to do with us living together."

"I'd advise you to—"

"No," Malcolm said coldly, with barely restrained anger. "I'd advise you to get the hell off my property before I throw your skinny ass off of it."

"Son-of-a—"

"Whoa!" Luther jumped in the space between his son and the stranger. "That's enough Mr. Madison. Serena's not here, so go on 'bout your business."

Malcolm and Zander stared each other down from opposite sides of Luther's body.

Zander turned and stalked down the stairs, shooting one last angry glare at Malcolm before he climbed into his Mercedes Benz and sped away.

"Serena better check her little *fiancé*," Malcolm spat, turning to stomp into the house.

Luther thought of Malcolm's immediate reaction to Serena's fiancé and smiled broadly. It had been a rather *revealing* exchange.

Serena was tired as all get out when she parked her car behind Malcolm's SUV in the driveway. The digital clock on the dash read 8:45 P.M. Another late night at the shop, working hard to make someone else money.

That would all end soon. She already started hinting to her regulars that she would be opening her own salon in the near future. She even had the name all picked out: Haiba Day Spa & Salon—*Haiba* was Swahili for beauty of character, countenance, or appearance.

Sighing, she grabbed her pocketbook from the passenger seat and exited her vehicle. A tub filled with steaming hot water was calling her name and she definitely planned on answering the call.

Serena had just entered the house when she heard a blend of male and female laughter float from the kitchen. Surprised, she paused, tensing as she listened for more.

"Oh, Malcolm you are *so* funny."

Serena's brow arched at the breathy sex-kitten voice. Now curious, she turned and headed in the direction of the kitchen. *Curiosity killed the cat*, she thought. *Yes, but satisfaction brought it back.*

She halted in the doorway, her eyes taking in the cozy scene before her. Malcolm was at the stove stirring in a large pot while his female companion, a rather buxom beauty whose breasts were defying gravity *and* reality, sat on the cushioned bench beneath the bay windows.

How . . . cozy.

Nothing but the devil made Serena force a fake smile and clear her throat. "Hello."

Malcolm glanced over his shoulder at her and his companion immediately turned wary eyes to Serena.

Serena felt instant dislike radiate from the woman. *Don't hate, heifer.*

"Yvonne, this is Serena, my ex-wife. Serena . . . Yvonne."

Serena walked toward her with an outstretched hand. "Nice to meet you—"

Yvonne pointedly ignored it and gave Serena a frigid smile that spoke volumes.

Serena raised a brow. *Oh no, this raggedy weave-wearing heifer didn't.* Deciding to have a little fun, she let her hand fall to her side as she dropped her purse on the countertop and moved over to Malcolm. He had completely missed the terse exchange between the women.

"I'm so hungry," Serena said huskily, moving so close to Malcolm that her breasts pushed lightly against his strong arm. She let her hand rest lightly on his lower back as she peered past him to look down into the pot. "Care to share?"

Malcolm's body tensed and he turned his head to look down at her. Because of her height, their mouths were just inches apart. "What are you up to, Serena?" he asked low in his throat.

Serena made her face the picture of innocence. "What?" she asked.

"Don't write a check you can't cash, Serena," he told her, his voice as dark and intense as his eyes.

Serena felt a shiver of some emotion race through her body.

"Should I leave you two alone?" Yvonne asked with attitude from behind them.

Immediately Serena stepped away from him, de-

ciding not to play with fire just for the sake of anger-
ing a woman she didn't know. "Enjoy your date,
Malcolm," she said in a harsh whisper, before walking away from him to pick up her purse and leave the
kitchen.

"Oh, your fiancé stopped by to see you."

Serena's steps momentarily paused at Malcolm's
words. *Fiancé? Zander came here?* She didn't even
bother to ask any questions. Right now she was hurt
by Malcolm's audacity to bring a date into the home
they shared. Okay, they weren't married, it wasn't
their home, and they weren't even friends. *But that's
not the point. Right?*

Growling in frustration and another emotion she refused to claim, Serena stomped up the stairs and
slammed her bedroom door behind herself with childish pleasure.

She wasn't angry just at Malcolm, she was dis-
pleased with herself as well. Against her wishes, her
conscious thought, her common sense, she wanted
Malcolm so badly that she thought she was going to
lose her mind.

Although they kept their distance, the mornings
were her undoing. Walking past his room as he did
his sit-ups bare-chested. The sight of him naked—save
for a damp towel that did nothing to hide the long,
throbbing member she remembered *all* too well. The
scent of his cologne as they each prepared their
own breakfast. The sight of how well his urban
clothes fit his tall muscular frame. All of it had her
sweating like a fiend at night.

Yes, if Serena had just met Malcolm for the first
time—without all of their marriage baggage—she'd
throw some rhythm his way so quick *both* his heads
would spin.

Serena tossed her purse onto the middle of the
bed. "Think, Serena. Remember," she prodded

herself, almost in a desperate chant as she paced the length of the room. She squeezed her eyes shut. "Remember what he did. Embrace the anger. *Where* is the damned anger?"

She yelped in frustration as she smacked her forehead with the palm of her hand.

Serena was not going to let one helluva body and sexy eyes make her forget that Malcolm Saint James was on her shit list for hurting her like no one ever had.

Squeak-squeak.

Malcolm heard the floorboards above his head squeak in an almost rhythmic pattern. The room above the kitchen was Serena's. He knew without question that she was pacing, something she did when she was either working out a problem or working off anger.

Yvonne reached across the island to stroke his hand with a soft and seductive smile. Malcolm took a sip of his wine and forced himself to smile back at her.

He met Yvonne a couple of years ago when he came to visit Mama James. They dated—and did some other things—during that two weeks. They had a good time together and stayed in contact. When he called her today and invited her over for dinner, he *knew* she would accept.

Although their dealings were casual, Yvonne didn't deserve to be used. He only invited her over because he was jealous of Serena having another man in her life.

Why should he care if Serena married someone else?

Why should his gut burn like fire at the thought of another man making love to her like he used to?

He dropped his fork back onto his plate of

spaghetti, drawing Yvonne's curious eyes. "Sorry," he said. "I . . . um . . . I shouldn't have—"

"This *is* an odd living situation, Mal," she said, nodding as she took a deep sip of wine. "And having dinner with a *friend* while your ex-wife is upstairs is even odder."

He said nothing as she stood and pushed her stool back. "Let's go to my place," she said softly with clear intent as she held her hand out to him.

Malcolm's hawklike eyes dropped to her hand. A decision had to be made. Another night in his bed flipping through the endless TV channels alone, or coming up with the shooting schedule alone, or eating dinner alone. Or . . .

Yvonne came around the island like a cat on the prowl and slid her hand up Malcolm's shoulder to turn him around on the rotating stool. She closed her eyes as she pressed her body between his open legs and wrapped her arms around his neck.

Malcolm tilted his chin up as Yvonne lowered her face to his. He could feel her sweet breath fan against his mouth just before her lips lowered to—

Squeak-squeak.

Malcolm jerked his head and upper body back from Yvonne as the floorboards went to singing. Serena was back on the move. "Um, Yvonne, I'm gone have to pass," he told her, slipping past her off his stool. "This just wasn't a good idea."

She looked anything but pleased as she gave him that sistah-girl cock of the head that could mean one of two things—the cold shoulder or the heat of a tongue lashing. Either way—even though he knew he probably deserved it—Malcolm wasn't in the mood.

"Yvonne, I—"

"Eh," she said shortly, holding up her hand.

"I apologize—"

"Eh . . . eh," she said again loudly.

Malcolm swallowed the rest of his words as she slid on her leather jacket and snatched up her purse.

"Don't call me no more," she sang sarcastically as she strode to the door.

The kitchen door closed firmly behind her.

Malcolm ran both his hands over his shiny bald head. Why in the world did he just ruin his night because of his ex-wife who was now engaged to someone else?

As kids they were as tight as two friends could be, but they foolishly crossed that line in their teens and completely derailed a friendship he missed. Serena had been adventurous, funny, and affectionate. He used to love the way she'd make him laugh and feel alive. Once she had made his chest feel light with all the love he had for her.

But all that changed once they moved in together. He now knew it was true that you never really knew a person until you lived together. Of course, he was also to blame for the failure of their marriage. Too young and cocky. Delusional with unrealistic stereotypes of male and female roles. Adamant that he was to be obeyed.

Hell, from the first time he met Serena she'd been feisty and strong. What made him think a wedding ring would change that?

Sighing in frustration, he started cleaning up the kitchen.

He wasn't surprised by the volume of anger Serena still had for him. Not that he blamed her. He was ashamed for his actions in the past and he could hardly blame her for her feelings. He had never thought of himself as a coward . . . except for that night. It had been years and she was just as venomous as if it all happened just yesterday.

He wanted to talk to her about their marriage—

their friendship, and hopefully come to some level of forgiveness from them both. He didn't want to reconcile—that was the last thing on his mind, but he wanted to disperse the anger and hard feelings they both had. They both were to blame, but the anger and resentment Serena exhibited was as if he was the only one at fault.

Over the years he had regrets. The older and wiser he got, the more regret he felt. Seeing Serena again took him back to that "place" right after their divorce where he questioned his actions and his motives.

Malcolm felt frustrated by the whole damn thing and resigned himself to a night of worrying over a marriage they both threw away.

Luther raised his hand to the front door of Elaine's beautiful colonial home. He was just about to ring the doorbell when he remembered the key that Elaine had pressed into his palm just one week earlier. *Lord, I love that woman,* he thought, as he reached into his pocket for his key ring.

And he did truly love her.

Malcolm constantly teased him for his *numerous* engagements. What could he say? He was a handsome and eligible bachelor with a damned good retirement income, all his own teeth, his own place, and two vehicles. Hell, he knew he was a hot commodity for women—and they knew it as well. Over the years he had gotten involved with a lot of beautiful and intelligent women who started hinting about marriage, straight out proposed marriage, or demanded the ring once the relationship progressed beyond six months.

He went through the motions with each and every one. And he knew he was wrong for that. A few he ended before they ever set a date, some during the wedding preparations, and only two got the "It's not you, it's me" speech the day before the wedding date. Each and every time he backed out quicker than a car going reverse doing seventy miles an hour.

There was Angela the stewardess, Yvette the waitress, Tara the bus driver, Mona the teacher, Donna the cashier, Miriam the non-profit CEO, and Karen, Sharonda, Harriet, Belinda, Naomi, Trisha, Sharon, Kimmie, and Reba. Yes, he remembered them all and something particular that he loved about each of them too—be it good sex or good cooking, but he never loved any of them enough to propose . . . until Elaine.

In the year they'd been dating, he'd discovered so many reasons to drop down on one knee and ask her to spend the rest of their lives together. Elaine was a combination of so many different things he loved in all of the women he had been involved with: she was good in the kitchen and the bedroom—sexist, but oh so true; she smelled wonderful; she laughed at his jokes; she listened to him; she talked to him; she asked his opinion; she was gracious, considerate, thankful, welcoming . . .

He could go on for days. He loved her and he was going to marry her. Even if no one believed him.

"Where are you, baby?" he hollered out as he entered the foyer and closed the front door behind him.

"Luther!" Elaine exclaimed, pleasure written all over her face as she came bounding toward him from the kitchen. "Miracle's coming!"

He engulfed her with his arms and pressed her body close to his, inhaling deeply of her scent. A scent that always made him feel invigorated. "Your daughter?" he asked, after kissing her warmly.

Elaine leaned back in Luther's arms, her hands on his shoulders as she rocked her hips gently with happiness. "Yes, my baby's coming home."

Miracle lived in Florida, and because of a new job hadn't been able to visit her mother for the last year.

"I say this calls for a huge family dinner. Time my boy met his new stepsister."

Elaine wiped the smudge of lipstick from Luther's lips with her thumb. "Not quite his stepsister yet."

Luther looked down at the beautiful, mature woman in his arms—and more importantly in his life, and his heart surged with love. "Soon, baby. Soon."

Chapter 5

Serena slowed her vehicle at a red light on Springfield Avenue. She reached for her cell phone in the passenger seat and dialed Zander's house number. The answering machine came on and she didn't bother to leave a message. She tried his cell phone next. When that didn't work, she dialed old reliable—his mama.

As the phone rang she thought of the purpose for her call. For the past two weeks, Zander aggressively pursued her. He came by the shop, he constantly called her cell phone, and his coming by Olivia's house claiming to be her fiancé was the final straw.

"Hello."

"Hi, Ms. Madison. Is Zander there, please?" Serena asked in her most polite voice.

"Hold on. Let me see if he's finished drinking his milk. Humph." The phone banged noisily against some hard object.

Serena's mouth fell open in astonishment. *He told his mama what I said?*

A horn blared loudly from behind and Serena shifted her eyes up to the rearview mirror to see the man in the vehicle behind her flipping her the bird. Her eyes shifted to the street light and saw the light was green.

"Hello?"

She pulled her car out of traffic, pulling into a parking spot. "Zander, this is—"

"Serena," he said with surprise in a low voice.

"I don't know if I should be more mad that you came by the house *or* that you told your mama what I said about her breast-feeding you."

"I don't know why you'd be mad about either one," he returned lightly.

"How did you find the house anyway?" she asked, glancing at the clock to be sure she wasn't going to be late for work.

Silence reigned and Serena felt suspicious. She repeated her question.

"Okay, okay, I followed you," he answered in a rush.

"You what?!"

"Look, I—"

"You know what, Zander. There's no feasible explanation for why you got in your car and trailed me *anywhere*, so I don't even want to hear it. Are you crazy or just silly?"

"*I'm* silly?" he asked in disbelief. "Come on now, Serena, you cut hair for a living."

No, he didn't.

"Zander, you accused me of trickin', you said your mama don't trust me, and you just called me stupid on the sly." Serena put on her left turn signal, eyeing the oncoming traffic in the side mirror as she held her phone to her face. "So why you acting like a stalker-in-training then?"

"I didn't mean—"

"Yes, you did."

He released a heavy breath.

"Can't we just go our separate ways and be adult about it?" she asked, pulling her vehicle into traffic.

"I just don't understand how after everything you told me about him you can agree to move back in with him." Zander said, sounding resigned. "I know you Serena, and you don't do anything, not for money or anything else, unless you *want* to. What? I gotta treat you bad for you to feel me like I feel you."

Serena's guilt flooded her in waves, but she had to be honest with him. "Zander, I made up my mind about us breaking up the night you proposed. Malcolm has nothing to do—"

"See there, baby, I told you she was scandalous."

Serena raised a brow at the sound of Ms. Madison's voice suddenly on the line.

"Mama? Hang up that phone," Zander hollered in the background.

"You ain't want no man's leftover's anyway. Her own husband ain't—"

"Mama!" Zander barked, cutting off the rest of her words.

Serena pulled her car to a stop at another of the endless lights lining the full length of Springfield Avenue. She started to cuss Zander *and* his mama out, but just hung up the phone instead. Her cell phone's ring tone, "My Boo" by Usher & Alicia Keyes, sounded almost immediately but Serena ignored it.

She wasn't in the mood for the drama Zander and his mama were trying to bring into her world, besides her mind was focused on the truth in Zander's words.

I know you Serena, and you don't do anything, not for money or anything else, unless you want to.

* * *

"Rise and shine, son."

Beneath his pillows Malcolm's face formed into a frown at the sound of his father's voice awakening him. Stretching beneath the covers, he flopped over onto his back, carelessly sending pillows dropping to the floor as he eyed his father sitting on the edge of the bed. "What time is it?" he asked, his voice heavy with sleep.

Luther looked down at his gold wristwatch. "Eleven A.M."

Malcolm groaned and covered his eyes with his steely forearm.

Luther rose and walked around the room that had been first his parents and then his mother's alone for so long after his father's death. He covered the sharp pain he felt with a joke. "Didn't know you liked pink ruffles boy," he teased, speaking of the frilly décor.

"Ha . . . ha . . . ha," Malcolm offered dryly, flinging the covers back from his body to rise and walk naked and unashamed across the room to his unpacked suitcases atop the dresser. "There's no need to change the décor because I'm headed on the first thing smoking back to New York when all this is over."

"I was hoping you'd decide to move back home, son."

Malcolm heard the regret in his father's tone, but he felt adamant about his decision. He looked over at the man who raised and loved him every day of his life. "My business is all set up there. New York's my home now, Pops."

"What 'bout the house?"

Malcolm pulled on crimson pajama bottoms. "I'm not going to sell it. You could live in it."

"Elaine and me?"

Malcolm laughed. "Yeah, sure. *If* you and Elaine make it down the aisle, ya'll can live here."

"First off, Elaine has a beautiful house in Montclair.

Secondly, *when* we marry I'll be moving out of my bachelor pad into her place."

"You giving up your apartment?" Malcolm asked in surprise.

Luther cleared his throat. "I didn't say all that," he said, and then had the nerve to smile sheepishly.

Malcolm cocked a mocking brow. "Sounds like a promising way to start a marriage."

"It's a sorry rat ain't got but one hole."

Malcolm just laughed.

Luther picked up Malcolm's Arriflex 16mm camera. He smiled with pride. He clearly remembered buying Malcolm his first camera. Of course his son had really wanted a video camera, but it had been way out of Luther's budget. So he bought the Polaroid instead and Malcolm hadn't even complained. He was a good kid and now he was an even better man.

"Mama would hold screening parties with all her church ladies whenever you had a new documentary," Luther said, picking up the costly camera to look through the lens.

"Yeah, she told me," Malcolm said. "I really miss her."

"Me, too." Luther forced a smile over the sadness as he sat the camera back in its case. "I came over here to tell you that Elaine and I are moving up the wedding date."

"For real?"

Luther beamed with love. "Her daughter, Miracle, is coming home for Thanksgiving and we're going to have it then so that both our kids can be there."

Malcolm looked surprised and locked his intense eyes with his father's. "You're really serious this time?"

"Serious as a heartache, son."

For the first time, Malcolm truly believed that his father was going through with a wedding. "Damn. Well, um, congratulations but that's in less than a month. Will it be enough time to get everything together?"

Luther laughed. "Boy, Elaine already started changing the plans. Oh, it's enough time. In fact, thought we'd go get fitted for our tuxes . . . if you're not busy."

Malcolm reached his hand out offering his father his fist. "Hey, I'm never too busy for my Pops."

Luther nodded and tapped his fist on top of his son's, giving him a pound. "That's my boy."

"Now ladies ya'll know I'm not lying. Men are called dogs because they'll hump anything, and the only thing on their mind is getting a bone or trying to find somewhere to bury a bone."

The ladies in the rinse area of the salon either agreed with Tawanda, one of Serena's regular clients, or playfully chastised her.

Serena just laughed as the outspoken and always entertaining woman held court.

"I hate to say it but she got a point," another client said, wearing a plastic cap as she waited for her rinse to set in. "I know I'd done had to send many a stray dog hunting for a new yard to poop in, *if* you know what I mean."

"Now, not all men are dogs, ladies," Evelyn chimed in from the front of the salon as she worked on a client's head.

"You know what I can't stand about men," said Mrs. Weathers, a woman in her mid-sixties who came to the shop weekly to get her hair washed, pressed, and rolled just like the old days.

"Preach, Mrs. Weathers," someone shouted.

Evelyn left her client in the chair to come and stand next to Mrs. Weather's chair. "I *got* to hear this."

"Men swear that a woman can't live without a

man. Now that's a bunch of mess. If you ask me, men can't live without a woman."

The ladies all cosigned that one.

"Now I love my Harold. And he loves me. We been married forty years, but I know if he goes on through the Pearly Gates before I do, I ain't looking for another man to have to play cook, maid, laundress, psychologist, accountant, and conscience for. No more." Mrs. Weathers removed the hand towel from her neck as she eyed the women watching her intently. "Now Harold. He'd remarry so quick that my head would spin in my grave. A man do not know how to function alone."

"She right 'bout that."

"You ain't never lied, Mrs. Weathers."

"You can't get them to admit that though."

The women's comments flooded together in the air above them.

"Most women—especially black women—don't need a man to step in and pick up the pieces. Hell, we been the ones carrying them pieces the whole time," Mrs. Weathers finished.

"Yeah but what about sex, Mrs. Weathers?" someone asked.

Mrs. Weather's rolled her eyes heavenward. "When you get my age the only big "O" you looking for is Oprah at four o'clock."

The ladies all roared with laughter.

"Yeah, but what about a younger woman, Mrs. Weathers?" Serena asked, as she motioned for Tawanda to come sit in her chair.

"Baby . . . if I got to tell you gals how to get the big "O" without a man in sight then *ya'll* the one need to watch Oprah. She tells you about them toys and things ya'll can buy these days."

The ladies all fell out in laughter.

"I'm like you, Mrs. Weathers." Serena looked over at the older woman. "When it comes to marriage, once is definitely enough for me."

Evelyn rolled her eyes before sashaying back to the front of the salon to her waiting client. "Chile, please, you're way too young to talk that foolishness."

"Had you a dog, huh?" Tawanda asked, turning to glance at Serena over her shoulder.

"Uh, no," Serena admitted, now wishing she had kept her comment to herself as all eyes turned on her.

"Had hand trouble?" Mrs. Weathers asked. "Stingy? Mean? Nasty?"

Again Serena shook her head. "No, ma'am."

Everyone looked confused.

"We were just too young. I got married when I was eighteen," Serena told them before their imaginations could run amuck.

"Is that that fine, bald brother who came in to see you last month?" Evelyn called back to Serena.

"Looks ain't everything," Serena grumbled as she started to comb down Tawanda's wrapped hair.

"Serena's ex fine, huh, Evelyn?" one of the ladies asked.

"Girl, Denzel, Morris, *and* Boris wrapped up in one kinda fine," Evelyn relayed to the ladies with relish.

Serena rolled her eyes heavenward as the majority of the women starting fanning themselves.

The women started debating on just who the sexiest actor was when the bell above the front door of the salon rang. Rasheed, the neighborhood independent salesman came in toting his almost suitcase-size duffel bag on one shoulder.

"Body oils, children toys, pocketbooks. You name it and I got it," Rasheed proclaimed, as he set his bag on the short glass table in the waiting area.

Evelyn shot him the evil eye. "You missed that big NO SOLICITATION sign on the door, Rasheed?"

"Uh-huh, sure did," he said with his usual flare. "Still want that *Beyond Paradise* by Estee Lauder body oil? Got a whole gift set—oil, bath wash and lotion— with your name all on it for the low, low price of . . . twenty dollars."

Evelyn met his stare. "Fifteen."

"Eighteen," he countered.

"Deal."

With that out of the way, Rasheed was back in business to sell his wares to the ladies. Even Mrs. Weathers bought a jack-in-the-box-like toy for her great-grandson.

Rasheed tried to talk Serena into buying a gorgeous—and impressive—knock-off Gucci bag. Serena refused. If she couldn't afford the real thing, she wasn't going to front with a fake Gucci that was for sure.

They were still debating the issue when the bell above the door rang again. A middle-aged woman with a beautiful face and kind smile walked into the salon. Serena knew that she was Luther's Elaine from a picture he showed her just last week.

"I am delivering savings to the urban community. Where else can you buy a two-thousand-dollar handbag for just fifty dollars?"

Serena used her arm to push past Rasheed and his spiel. "Elaine?" she asked.

The woman smiled in surprise. "Yes . . . yes, I'm Elaine and you're Serena, right? I can tell from all the pictures at Mama James' house."

"Nice to meet you," Serena said, taking Elaine's offered hand. "Guess I should thank you. Malcolm said you got the room at the house together for me."

Elaine smiled. "I'm glad you like it. Is there somewhere we can talk in private?"

"Oh, sure." Serena led the way back to the break room.

"Okay, Miss Siddity . . . thirty-five dollars for a genuine imitation Gucci," Rasheed hollered to Serena just as she closed the door to the break room behind Elaine.

"Genuine imitation?" Elaine asked, laughing.

Serena just shook her head. "How can I help you, Elaine?"

"Well, Luther and I have decided to move the wedding date up to Thanksgiving weekend."

Serena thought of Luther's track record with weddings but smiled warmly anyway. "Congratulations."

"Save the congrats if he actually goes through with it." Elaine reached in the pocket of her wool blazer and pulled out a dollar bill. She smiled at Serena over her shoulder as she purchased a fruit juice from the vending machine. "I know about all the fiancées."

It was Serena's turn to be surprised. "Are you a little—"

"Worried?" Elaine supplied with a smile. She shook her head. "Not at all because either way Elaine gone be all right. I have never let a man faze me, including Luther. Oh, in my younger days I'd lose sleep behind some man, wondering who, when, where, why, and how. Even used to get out my bed three in the morning and drive around town looking for my M.I.A. man of the moment. Age and wisdom have cooled me. I got my own house, my own money, and my own way of doing things. So when it comes to Luther actually saying I do: if he do he do, if he don't he don't."

Serena liked her and wished she could be as nonchalant. "I think Luther knows a good thing when he sees it."

Elaine took a healthy swig of her drink. "He better."

"What can I do for you?" Serena asked, remembering Tawanda and her half-curled hair.

"Luther told me you're a beautician and we both thought it would be a good idea to get you to do the hair for the bridal party."

"Wouldn't your own beautician mind that?" Serena asked.

"Chile please, I haven't been to a hair salon in decades. This rod and set is a homemade hairdo."

"Good job," Serena admitted, sticking her hands in the pocket of her black barber's cape.

"On my wedding day I don't want to do a thing but show up and look good. So will you do it?"

"No problem."

"I'm not gone hold you up." Elaine screwed the cap back on her bottle of fruit juice. "Besides I have so much to do to get this wedding together. I haven't even found somewhere to have the ceremony."

"You know Malcolm and I got married in the backyard at the house."

Elaine looked thoughtful and then inspired. "You know it is a *beautiful* backyard and it's much much bigger than that little patio I have at my house. I'm sure he doesn't care if its at a church or a dollar store. We could rent a tent. Do you think Malcolm would mind?"

Serena shrugged. "I can't see why he would mind, but you'll have to ask him. I stopped guessing on the way Malcolm's mind works a long time ago."

Elaine focused wise eyes on Serena. "Do you mind if I ask how it's going at the house? I know it can't be easy."

"It's cool," Serena lied. "You know he does his thing and I do mine."

"There is no amount of money I would've accepted to move in with my ex, but he was what I like to call Triple A. An abusive a-hole with an attitude."

"Malcolm and I never had any drama like that. Just too young mostly. I'm sorry, but I don't know too many people 'round these parts who will turn up their nose at twenty-five grand." Serena couldn't help sounding defensive.

"I didn't mean it that way, Serena." Elaine reached to clasp Serena's hand warmly. "Luther told me what all he knew about the breakup."

Serena felt warm with the shame of others knowing and discussing what Malcolm did.

"Actually, Luther thinks you two could make it again if you both wanted to."

"Oh no, definitely not." Serena said with anger brimming in her eyes.

"Can I share some wisdom?"

Uh-oh, here we go. "Yes, ma'am."

"Sometimes when you forgive others for pain that they've caused, you free yourself. All that anger and hurt you continue to carry weighs down on you, just wearing you down physically and mentally." Elaine winked at Serena. "I forgave my ex-husband's affairs, abuse, and neglect. Not for him, but for me. Even before I signed those divorce papers, I forgave him. I released the anger and in the process released myself from the baggage. Forgive, Serena, even if you can't forget."

Elaine reminded Serena of her Auntie and she felt sad because she missed the wisdom and the love of her aunt. When Auntie passed away from throat cancer just three months after Serena married Malcolm, she knew she would forever feel the loss.

"You know my, uh, my Aunt Vanessa—I called her Auntie—she raised me after Mom died. Auntie, um . . . she would've told me the same thing."

"So you know I'm not lying." Elaine turned and

reached for the door handle. "Just something to consider, Serena."

"Yes, ma'am."

After she was gone, Serena wrapped her arms around herself. Forgive Malcolm? Was she that mentally mature to release all the anger she'd been clutching like an emotional raft all these years?

Better said than done.

Interlude

On Bended Knee

1994

"Serena? Serena, Malcolm's here to see you."

Serena shrugged her shoulders, but then felt bad for acting insolent towards her beloved Auntie. It wasn't Auntie's fault that she was straight trippin' over some "he say she say" her friend Monique told her about Malcolm.

Monique and her family moved in next door last year. Serena found the girl lively and fun-spirited. They became friends instantly.

Serena looked up at her aunt standing in the doorway of her bedroom and smiled at the only mother she ever knew. "I'm coming," she said, rising from her bed and using the remote to turn off the rerun of *Martin* on the television.

Monique said that she saw Malcolm—*her* Malcolm, talking to Reesie, the school's resident hoochie in an empty hallway at school. Never had she had a reason to doubt that Malcolm loved her and he'd never cheated on her—not once . . . until now.

Serena studied her reflection in the full-length

mirror on the back of her bedroom door. She pulled the braided extensions, that reached the small of her back, up into a ponytail and smoothed her hands over her oversized Levi overalls.

All the boys thought Reesie's well-developed body was slammin' and were sweatin' her all the time. Foolishly, she had thought her Malcolm was different. And he was, wasn't he?

Serena left her room and jogged down the stairs. Halfway into the dimly lit den, she paused in her steps and her mouth shaped into a "O" with surprise and pleasure.

She sighed as she came closer to the display. Rose petals and tiny votive candles were arranged in a huge heart shape in the center of the room. Individual chocolate candies, each with a letter atop it, spelled out "Be My Date 4 Prom?" in the center of the heart.

"You like it, Serena?"

Serena turned at the sound of Malcolm's husky voice and squealed with excitement. "Aw Malcolm, this is the bomb," she said softly, as she embraced him.

It was the kind of sweet gestures that Malcolm always did to let her know he loved her just as much as she loved him. Serena just assumed they were going to the prom together, but for him to make an effort like this made her love him even more.

Serena leaned back in his arms and smiled up at his face. He was handsome. He was sweet. He was kind. And he was all hers. To hell with Monique's gossip.

Serena leaned forward, pressing her lips and her body to his. She was loving the way his heart pounded wildly against her chest as their tongues tangoed. There was an electricity between them. An almost silent buzz of awareness that kept them both intensely drawn to each other.

Malcolm's strong hands rose with comfort and

familiarity to cup Serena's bottom and slowly grind his lengthening erection against her.

Serena tingled with warmth and pleasure, the bud between her thighs swelling and moistening in desire for this man that she loved desperately.

Their love was honest and real. And although they both wanted each other with an intensity, they made the decision to wait. Still, it was harder and harder to ignore that buzz.

"Ahem, do I have to throw water on you two?" Auntie mused from behind them.

Malcolm and Serena jumped apart. Serena flushed with embarrassment and Malcolm strolled away as slowly as he could to take a seat before Auntie saw just how hot he was.

"Look Auntie, it's dope, right?" Serena asked, reaching for her aunt's hand to pull her closer to Malcolm's handiwork.

Auntie cocked a brow. "And dope means good, right?"

Malcolm and Serena laughed.

"Yes, Ms. Freeman," Malcolm offered, shifting to sit up and prop his elbows on his knees.

"Ya'll know I don't talk that street talk." Auntie swatted at them both with the hand towel she held.

As they all began talking about preparations for the upcoming prom, Serena and Malcolm kept looking at each other and smiling softly with love.

One Month Later

As the soft refrains of R. Kelly's "Bump & Grind" faded into the background to be replaced by Heatwave's R&B classic "Always and Forever," Malcolm pulled Serena into his embrace.

"You look good as hell, Serena," he whispered in

her ear. And he meant that. He was pleased and surprised by her strapless pale-pink dress when he picked her up earlier that evening.

"You, too," she whispered back, closing her eyes to inhale deeply of the scent of his Polo cologne as they rocked together and admired his freshly cut high-top fade.

"Did you have fun tonight?" he asked, his stomach warm with nervousness.

"I loved everything. The limo, the food, the music, your company. Everything was real nice. Thank you."

"Good," he said, raising his hand from her hip to wipe away the beads of sweat on his upper lip. "I really want tonight to be special."

Serena looked up at Malcolm. "What's wrong? Is everything okay?"

The spotlight that drifted around the room all night suddenly fell on them and Serena started in surprise as all eyes turned in their direction. She watched in horror as everyone moved back to form a circle around them.

Her eyes drifted around the room at the many faces. She saw Monique shoot her a questioning look. Serena just shrugged as Heatwave tearing up that song lowered to a much softer level.

Malcolm slowly dropped to one knee and took her hand in both of his. His heart pounded wildly in his chest and he felt slightly nauseous, but there was nothing more he wanted to do at that moment. He smiled up at Serena as her eyes glassed over and she started trembling.

"Serena, you and I started out as friends—best friends, but ever since that night we first kissed in your backyard, I knew I wanted and needed you in my life as more than just my friend. I love you. I love the hell outta you, Serena."

Tears streamed from Serena's eyes as she focused on

Malcolm and nothing else. Not the chattering of their classmates. Not the snide comments flung into the wind by a few immature boys. Not even the sighs of sweet pleasure by nearly all the girls. Nothing but Malcolm, and his words, his feelings, his touch.

Malcolm released Serena's hand as he reached into the pocket of his tuxedo and extracted a small, gold cardboard box. He opened it and pulled out the simple but beautiful eighth-of-a-carat diamond engagement ring.

He licked his lips and placed the band on the tip of her left ring finger, before looking up at her with all of the love and devotion he had for her. "Serena Freeman, I can't imagine spending my life with anyone but you." He took a deep steadying breath. "Will you marry me?"

The small hint of uncertainty in his voice tempered by the love, caused Serena's heart to burst with love for her man. Her future husband. "Yes, baby. Yes. Yes," she whispered, as he slid the ring onto her slender finger and rose to kiss the tears from her cheeks before capturing her full mouth in a sweet and endearing kiss that quickly deepened.

The circle around them shrunk as the classmates surged forward with congratulations and curiosity.

Chapter 6

"You look like death warmed over."

Serena felt like it, but she didn't exactly need to hear it from Malcolm. She didn't know if it was a cold or the flu, but one of the two was kicking her behind like she stole something. She called in sick to work and succumbed to her bed. Nearly two hours later she woke up so thirsty she thought she'd swallowed sawdust. She had dragged herself downstairs into the kitchen to get ice water.

"Are you sick?" Malcolm asked, covering his mouth with the turtleneck of his bulky burnt-orange sweater.

Serena shot him a nasty glare as she washed her hands at the kitchen sink. "I'm gonna cough on your pillow," she said, wiping her hands before she filled a glass with ice cubes from the freezer. She hated how much it hurt her throat to talk.

"Ha ha, real funny," he said, watching her closely.

Serena moved back to the sink to fill the glass with water, which she immediately drank greedily, hoping to quench the inferno raging inside her body.

She felt like she burned with fever and was wracked

with chills all at one miserable time. Her shoulders felt weighted by two-ton dumbbells. Although she just woke up, all she wanted to do was go back to sleep.

"You really should get back in bed," Malcolm offered.

"No shit, Sherlock," she snapped, filling her glass again. She shot Malcolm another annoyed look as she dragged out of the kitchen. She had to pause at the bottom of the steps, clutching the ornate banister as she tried to gather enough strength to fight her way back to bed. Whatever ailed her was knocking her out for the count.

Unable to fight the weakness, Serena slumped down on the bottom step, her unsteadiness causing the chilled water to slosh out of the glass and soak the arm of her robe. She breathed heavily, trying to keep the contents of her stomach down. She groaned in misery, letting her eyes drift closed for a few precious seconds.

"Come on, Serena," Malcolm said huskily.

Serena opened her eyes, surprised by his sudden appearance as he took the glass from her hand to set on a table in the foyer. "I'm okay, Mal—"

"No, you're not," he admonished with just a hint of a smile, bending down with a pensive face to pick her limp body up into his able arms with no effort.

"You're a bully, Malcolm Saint James," she murmured against his neck, her eyelids heavy with sleep.

"And you were sleeping on the stairs," he pointed out.

"Was not."

"Was to."

"You been getting on my nerves since we were eight years old."

"Same here."

Malcolm set his laptop on the bed and rose from the club chair, his eyes locked on the window in surprise. He pushed his hands in the pockets of his corduroy pants as he walked over to his bedroom window and leaned against the sill. He gazed out at the fine layer of white covering the rooftops, cars, and the sidewalk outside.

He smiled as two kids came racing down the stairs of the house across the street to play in what little snow had accumulated. They futilely gathered up snow to make snowballs, the laughter and joy obvious on their faces.

Bet my snowgirl will be way better than your snowman, Saint James.

It was amazing the moments in time the mind kept or discarded. As Serena's words floated to the forefront of his memories from a place nearly twenty years ago, he could clearly remember when she'd spoken them.

It had been one of the worst snowstorms the east coast had seen in over a decade. Malcolm and Serena had been just nine years old and ecstatic because school was cancelled. They spent the entire day frolicking in the snow, even as the cold seeped past their layers of warm clothing. Only Mama James admonishing them to come in for lunch could put a halt to their snowball fights, angel making and snowman— or snowgirl—making contest.

Malcolm laughed lightly at the memory, turning away from the window to leave the room. He wanted to check on his patient. It had been over two hours since he spiked the lemon tea he made her with Thera-Flu. He knew Serena absolutely hated taking medicine.

He knocked on her bedroom door and waited for a response. When nothing but silence followed, Malcolm cracked the door open. Serena was laying on her back spread eagle, the bedcovers mostly on the floor, her mouth ajar.

Malcolm walked in the room and stood by her bed

to look down at her sleeping form. Her auburn hair was pulled back from her face. Her cheekbones were high and regal above the most luscious lips that were plump and begging to be kissed. Eyes that were shielded by closed lids were a shade of ebony that he could never forget. Her skin reminded him of cinnamon. Her pajama top was slightly ajar and he could just detect the curve of her full breast teasing him until his hand ached to caress her there. His loins hardened in a rush of desire that was as fierce as the first days of their marriage. He thought she was absolutely beautiful and serene . . . until she began to snore softly.

He frowned deeply at the sounds of her congestion filling the room. "Works better than a cold shower," he said dryly, even though his awareness of her did not ease.

There was an ever-constant hum of electricity between them ready to spark into an explosive anger or electrifying passion. Ten years and Serena was still in his blood.

How easy he fell back into the role of her caretaker. At the sight of Serena weak and fatigued at the bottom of the steps he hadn't hesitated in taking care of her. He wanted to do it because a woman like Serena—strong and independent—would only succumb to fatigue like that if she was sick.

Noticing a fine sheen of perspiration on her upper lip and brow, Malcolm left the room to retrieve clean bed linens and a fresh pitcher of ice water. Back in the room, he scooped her up gently into his arms and set her on the chaise longue in the corner. She murmured something unintelligible in her sleep but did not awaken.

Quickly he changed the bed linens, even down to the pillows, and then he took the liberty of looking through her things for clean pajamas. He paused as he picked up a pale-pink lace teddy. With a roguish grin, he pictured the delectable item on her svelte body; then he replaced that and grabbed cotton PJs that were more sensible.

He stripped her quickly, knowing she would scald him with that infamous tongue of hers if she woke up before he was done. Although he was curious about any changes in Serena's body since they last made love, he wasn't a horny lecher looking to peep out some T & A. Besides, his awareness and attraction to Serena was something he wanted to fight and he didn't want the sight of her naked body branded on his brain. So he dressed her as fast as he could and tried to think neutral thoughts.

He scooped her up again, concerned as she shivered and nestled closer to the warmth of his body. He was acutely aware of a plush breast pressed intimately against his chest.

Malcolm brushed the hair from her face and pulled the fresh covers up to her chest as she breathed heavily in sleep. As he watched her, something so familiar that he hadn't allowed himself to feel in years tugged at his heart, and Malcolm knew that if he didn't guard it better that he would be in big trouble.

He crossed the room to sit on the chaise longue, intermittently watching Serena and then the snow falling outside.

Serena awakened surrounded by the feel of cool crisp sheets. She sighed in pleasure, burying her face deeper into the pillows.

"Stop playing possum, Serena."

She frowned at the sound of Malcolm's bemused voice. She opened her eyes to find him sitting across the room in the chaise. "You enjoying seeing me sick so much you needed a ringside seat?" she asked him, her voice hoarse.

Malcolm rose with a digital thermometer in hand. "Think you can open your mouth without a wisecrack coming out?"

"Go to—"

Malcolm slid the thermometer into her mouth with ease and a devilish glint in his eyes. "Under your tongue, Serena," he instructed like she was a child.

"Why are you—"

"No . . . no . . . no," he chastised, enjoying her inability to speak.

Serena shifted the thermometer under her tongue and clamped her mouth shut, staring up at the ceiling as she did.

Beep . . . beep . . . beep.

Malcolm removed the thermometer before she could, reading the results. "One hundred point four."

Serena made a face. "No wonder I'm burning up inside. I hate being sick."

"I know." Malcolm told her, moving around the bed to the nightstand to fill her glass with some of the ice water from the pitcher. "I called a good doctor friend of mine and he said to give you as much fluid as you could tolerate to keep from dehydrating."

"Why are you being so nice to me?" she croaked with a wince as she eyed him warily.

"Always had a weakness for strays," he shot over his shoulder before exiting the room.

Serena wished she had the strength to throw her pillow at his head. She was just coming to the realization that her pajamas were changed when Malcolm backed into the room carrying a tray.

"Who changed my pajamas? You?"

Malcolm looked at her like she was crazy as his steps faltered briefly. "No it was your fairy godmother," he muttered with sarcasm. "Who else do you think changed them?" His voice was exasperated.

Serena's eyebrows furrowed together into a frown. "What?"

"Can you sit up?" Malcolm asked, ignoring her question as he felt the cool winds of an argument fill the air.

Serena pulled her body to a sitting position, her eyes locked on him. "You—"

"You were soaked with sweat, I changed your pajamas . . . stop stressing, Serena," he told her darkly as he leaned in close to her to place the tray holding a bowl of chicken noodle soup across her lap. "You act like I never saw you naked before."

"Doesn't mean you get to see me naked whenever you want to," she snapped, looking down at the food sitting before her.

Malcolm just laughed. "If you've seen one set of T & A, you've seen them all."

Serena thought of Yvonne's gravity-defying breasts as she stirred her soup. "Just because my breasts don't stand at attention even when I'm lying down doesn't mean they're chop liver, Saint James."

Malcolm bent over to lock his eyes with hers. "You want me to tell you that you have an extraordinarily beautiful body, Serena?" he asked huskily.

She swallowed over a lump in her throat as her heart skipped to an erratic pattern that she wasn't altogether sure was safe. "I couldn't care less what you think," she retorted. "I am quite aware of my God-given attributes, thank you very much."

"Oh, does your little fiancé boost your ego?" he mocked.

"Little is definitely not a good nickname for him, that's for sure," she answered him boldly, not even bothering to explain that Zander and she were not engaged.

Malcolm's eyes sparkled. "Is he a better lover than me, wildcat?"

Serena flushed at his use of his old pet name for her. "*He's* the best I ever had," she lied.

"Yeah, right," he crowed, filled with his own bravado.

"Zander's loving is that of a grown man and not a fumbling, inept boy just learning what to do," she taunted before swallowing a spoonful of the broth.

Malcolm flung his bald head back as he laughed from deep in his gut. "A lie ain't nothing to tell, Serena."

"I never had an orgasm until I got into Zander's bed," she continued to lie with no shame. She wanted to hurt Malcolm's feelings the way he hurt hers all those years ago. It felt good to bring him down a peg or two.

"I gave as good as I got."

"You got the best I could muster in such a . . . *brief* time." Serena gave him a slow once over with her eyes. "I'd blink and it was over."

"Shrew."

"Minute Man."

"I used to have you climbing the walls."

"Yes . . . to get away."

Malcolm uncrossed his arms and clapped . . . slow and deliberate. "If you were faking you deserve an Oscar. Either way, I got me, you shoulda got you."

He turned and left the room before she could release some acerbic quip.

Serena felt the soup she ate going in reverse. She clapped her hand over her mouth and tried to breathe deeply to keep the contents of her stomach where it belonged . . . in her stomach. Serena didn't have the strength to walk, but she had to get to the bathroom.

She slid off the side of the bed to the floor and crawled on her hands and knees out of the bedroom as fast as she could. She winced as she struggled not to throw up . . . yet. She just made it to the bathroom in time, hugging the commode as she retched uncontrollably.

Suddenly Malcolm was kneeling at her side, flushing the commode as he grabbed a washcloth to wipe the sweat from her brow. "Not quite ready for food, huh?" he asked with compassion.

Serena shook her head, shivering and ashen. She hated that she slumped against him with such ease, but she was too weak to do anything else. She was even grateful when Malcolm gathered her into his arms and carried her back into her bedroom.

He gently laid her on the bed and pulled the covers up to her chin. "You okay now?" he asked, looking down at her with bemused eyes.

"Sleepy and in need of a Tic-Tac, but okay," she told him dryly as she shifted onto her side on the bed.

Malcolm smiled. "Still the comeback queen."

Serena snuggled her aching body down deeper beneath the covers, as she succumbed to the sleep her ailing body craved. "Thank you for taking care of me, Malcolm," she said softly, almost reluctantly.

"You're welcome." He walked to the door, pulling it open wide to leave open. "By the way . . . you still have a beautiful body."

Serena's eyes shot open at Malcolm's softly spoken words just before he left the room.

Malcolm was jolted from his sleep at the shocking feel of cold linens pressed against his skin. He lifted his head from the pillow, cloaked by the darkness, and saw his breath form in the air illuminated by the faint light of the moon.

He was cold. The house was cold. Gone was the

toasty warmth generated by the heater when he checked on Serena and then went to bed around ten.

Malcolm flung back the covers and immediately felt the chill cling to his nude, muscular frame. He shivered as he walked over to the window to see the rooftops of the houses and the street completely blanketed with snow that was still falling quite heavily.

"Damn," he swore, pulling on the corduroy pants he'd discarded earlier. He zipped the pants carefully, mindful that he wore no underwear, and then yanked on his sweater.

Malcolm flipped the switch and frowned when the light failed to appear. No lights and no heat. With the weather and it being the dead of night, he knew he wouldn't be able to get someone in to check everything out until the next day.

If he was this cold, then Serena, in her sick state, had to be miserable.

Malcolm slipped on a tight-fitting sweater cap to cover his bald head and rushed to pull on socks. "Shit, it's cold," he complained, being sure to keep his body moving as he slid on his pair of athletic sandals by the closet door.

"I need a flashlight," he said aloud to himself, suddenly remembering the mini version of one hanging on his key chain. Malcolm worked his way over to his dresser and felt around until his hands touched the cold metal of his keys.

With that tiny beam of light leading the way, Malcolm made his way to Serena's room. His heart ached to see her huddled into a tight ball in the center of the bed deep underneath the covers. "Serena. Serena, you awake?" he asked, not at all sure why he was whispering.

"Who could sleep in this oversized freezer?"

Malcolm laughed at her mumbled reply. "I think there's something wrong with the boiler and the electricity," he said, moving to grab the afghan from the back of the chaise to throw across her.

Serena peeked her head from under the covers and Malcolm thought she looked like a turtle. "Malcolm, I'm so cold," she admitted softly, her teeth chattering.

"I got an idea," he said. "Get back under the covers. I'll be right back."

Still using his trusty flashlight, he dipped into his room and snatched all of the covers from his bed and inside the chest at the foot of the bed. Malcolm carefully made his way down the stairs and into the den. He yelped in pain as his shin connected with the corner of the low-slung coffee table. Swearing, he shifted more to the right and directed the flashlight lower.

Once he reached the fireplace, he dropped the covers and grabbed the box of matches on the mantle, setting out quickly to get a fire going. Soon the first flicker of the fire's ember cast an orange glow on his triumphant face. Even that minimal amount of heat felt good to him and he knew a roaring fire would feel divine to Serena.

Quickly he worked to make a soft pallet of the covers a short distance from the fire. Satisfied that it was as comfortable as he could make it, Malcolm headed back upstairs to Serena's bedroom.

He immediately bent to gather her up into his arms.

"I can walk, Mal—"

"Just hold on, Serena," he ordered, handing her the flashlight to hold.

Carefully he made his way back downstairs and was surprised by the hesitance he felt to release Serena from his grasp. She felt just as good and right in his arms as she had in the past. A perfect fit. That scared him because he knew how deeply his feelings for Serena once ran.

Shaking off those familiar tugs at his heart, Malcolm lowered Serena to the blankets. "Thank you, Malcolm," she sighed with pleasure. "That fire feels so good."

"I'll call someone in the morning to get the heat and lights back on," he told her, rising to move over to the couch across the room.

"Okay," she answered softly, the sound of sleep already filling her voice.

He pulled the lone blanket he saved for himself over his body as he tried to shift into a comfortable position on the pretty—but dainty—Elizabethan-styled sofa. The sofa was about five feet long while he was six-foot-four.

Long, torturous minutes ticked by and Malcolm still felt shaky. He knew if he turned in his sleep he'd be on the floor. With a shake of his head, he looked over at Serena now sleeping peacefully on the comfy pallet. She slept on her side, leaving half the pallet—that was as wide as a queen sized bed—unused. The warm and cozy glow of the crackling fire illuminated her body while he just barely felt the heat of the fire radiating over to him.

As his legs hung awkwardly off the sofa, the covers looked as divine and tempting to him as a whorehouse would to a just-released prisoner. *Hell with it,* he thought, flinging away his cover. He kicked off his sandals and walked over to lie down beneath the covers with a small grunt of pleasure.

The only sound in the room was Serena's light snores and the crackle of the fire. Malcolm's eyes darted down to Serena as she shifted on her side and faced the fire, which meant her bottom, one he knew to be deliciously round and soft, would be pressed against his side. He tensed.

The sleep flew from Malcolm, to be replaced by an aching awareness of the woman lying beside him.

This was a rather romantic scene save for the fact that they were divorced, Serena was engaged to another man, and neither wanted to touch a relationship between them with a ten-foot pole. Still, he'd have to be blind and stupid to not notice just how damned sexy she was. With his noticing came awareness, and with the awareness came a desire to fulfill the physical hunger she filled him with.

Okay, fine, he was man enough to admit it. He wanted to make love to Serena so badly that just the thought of her body beneath him—or above him—as he filled her with his heat made him harder than a steel bat.

Malcolm would gladly make love to his ex-wife until she purred his name and let loose that little delicious hum she would make whenever she was pleased. He wanted to stroke deeply inside of her. He wanted to make her remember the passion they once shared. Touch. Stroke. Caress. *Satisfy*.

He shifted his body away from hers as much as he could without being off the pallet completely.

Seducing his ex-wife was not a part of his plans . . . no matter how good he *knew* it would be.

He counted sheep, forced his eyes to stay shut, tried to breathe deeply. *Anything* to go to sleep where he could hopefully escape the desire to strip those insanely childish PJs from Serena's body and kiss every inch of her.

He released a harsh breath and bit his fist as Serena turned in her sleep and pressed herself to the side of his body. All of the blood left his brain and rushed to his member, lengthening it like a long balloon being filled with air.

Her breast pushed against his side, her thigh straddled his legs, her warm hand nuzzled his neck. She purred softly in her sleep and it sounded like the moans of a woman being made love to. That did it.

The dam broke. All hell broke loose. He lost all reason, shifting his body to face hers. "Serena . . ."

She murmured in pleasure as she felt strong, warm, and familiar hands lightly touch her breasts and tease her aching nipples. As she was lifted from her sleep by his voice and his hands, she *knew* it was Malcolm touching her.

She gasped at the first feel of his tongue drawing delicate circles around her chocolate aureole with seductive effortlessness. His hands sought and found the throbbing bud between her quivering thighs and she whimpered in helpless desire. This was that enormous passion that always simmered there between them. It was familiar, it was delicious, it was wanted.

Malcolm was lost in his need of Serena. He nearly shook with the desire to bury himself deeply within her. The taste, scent and feel of her was just as he remembered. The way his heart raced and his loins hardened was like nothing he had experienced since their split. It felt right.

"Your body feels so good, Serena," he whispered against her cleavage as he kissed a hot trail to her other breast.

Serena opened her eyes and looked down at him as he lowered his bald head to draw her rock-hard nipple deeply into his mouth. She gasped and arched her back, raising her hands to press his head closer to her. "Oh, Malcolm," she whispered, amazed that the fire between them still burned with such intensity.

Passion overruled sensibility. Desire fought and won the battle over common sense. It had been years since she felt so alive and so vibrant from the touch of a man. No one had made her feel this way. No one but Malcolm.

He teased Serena's nipple with his clever tongue,

enjoying the feel of her body shivering beneath him. His hands lowered to tug the pajama pants down over her hips.

Serena raised her hips to assist him, immediately opening her legs as soon as they were free. When she felt the first stroke of his thumb against the throbbing bud between her legs without the barrier of her clothes, Serena released a shaky breath that spoke volumes of the pleasure he gave her.

Malcolm rolled away from Serena to shed himself quickly of his clothes and he enjoyed how her eyes stroked him. Anxious to feel his skin next to hers, he hurried back to lie on top of her. For long, precious, and uncountable moments they just reveled in enjoying the feel of each other. Serena massaged the hard contours of his back, the smooth baldness of his heads, the perfection of his buttocks. Malcolm stroked her breasts, massaged the contours of her thighs, and pressed his fingers into the full swell of her buttocks.

They both were nearly breathless from it all.

As Malcolm kissed and stroked every inch of her body, he wondered if there was anything that tasted as divine. He doubted it.

"Your body is beautiful, Serena," he heralded, as he sat back between her legs and feasted on her frame as the fire cast a soft glow upon it.

Malcolm's erection leaned heavy and awkward away from his body and he used strong hands to open Serena's legs wider before him. He licked his lips in anticipation and locked his dazed eyes with her own as he stroked her wetness with skill.

Serena flung her head back in abandon and arched her hips up to intensify his touch. Every bit of the way his fingers circled and rubbed and pressed upon her clitoris made her nearly blind, deaf and dumb. All she knew was his touch. All she smelled was his cologne. All she saw was him. All she heard were his moans and grunts of pleasure.

"Malcolm. Oh, baby, I'm gone come," she whimpered as she hotly licked her lips and raised her hands to squeeze and tease her own breasts.

Malcolm felt his shaft lengthen and swell even more at her wild abandon. This was the same Serena he knew so well. Nothing had changed. It had only intensified.

He continued the same slow circular motion against her bud and felt her core become wetter. He wanted her to come. He wanted to *make* her come.

Malcolm dropped to the floor on his stomach and jerked Serena closer to him by her hips. He growled as he lowered his head and replaced his fingers with his mouth, sucking deeply on the swollen bud and enjoying the heady taste of her.

The first spasm of release shocked Serena and she quivered uncontrollably as Malcolm continued his relentless pursuit of her pleasure. His tongue flickered the bud with agility and speed causing her to gasp and shout and scream his name as she thrashed her arms wildly on the floor.

"Taste good, baby," he moaned heatedly against her flesh. "So damn good."

Unable to take the pleasure she tried to inch away from his mouth but Malcolm just used one strong hand to lock her into place as he took the whole of her core into his mouth for one helluva French kiss that caused tears to well in her eyes.

For long, aching, but oh-so-pleasurable moments, Serena rode one wave after the next of her climax. When she finally slackened with the final waves of her release, her breathing was harsh and her heart pounded hard in her chest.

Malcolm kissed her there one last time before letting his head fall softly against her thigh.

"Good, baby?" he asked huskily as he pierced her with his eyes.

Serena nodded, still trying to gain some semblance of composure.

He shifted on his side and began to massage the aching length of his member, using a bit of his own small release to lubricate his hand. He reached for his pants and removed his wallet all with one hand. Quickly he removed a condom from the wallet and sheathed himself with ease.

He shifted to kiss a trail from Serena's toes to her shapely thighs. At the vee of her legs he inhaled deeply of *her* scent and wanted her even more. He moved up to capture a hard nipple in his mouth as Serena raised her hands to massage his shoulders.

"That was so good, Malcolm," she told him, wanting him deep and hard inside of her.

Malcolm looked up into her eyes. "Your fiancé ever make you come like that?" he asked huskily.

Serena's eyes shifted in a second from dazed desire to confusion and then finally anger. "Is that what this is to you? A competition?" she asked, effectively hiding the hurt from her voice.

Malcolm grimaced at his mistake. "Don't, Serena," he said softly, not wanting the moment—or the night—to end.

Serena closed her eyes as he attempted to clasp her tightly to him with his strong arms. "He's not my fiancé anyway, so you can give up your quest to be Billy Big Di—"

"Serena."

"Let me go, Malcolm. I don't know what the hell I was thinking anyway. After everything we've been through the last thing we need is a booty call for old times' sake."

"Serena—"

Serena felt all of her insecurities and the pain from

so many years ago swamp her. They were emotions she had long since tried to bury, but at that moment she felt strangled by them. "Malcolm, please," she pleaded, hating the raw emotion in her voice and the tears filling her eyes.

Oh, shit. Malcolm saw the pain in the eyes and heard it in her voice and he knew it had nothing to do with what almost happened tonight but everything to do with the end of the marriage ten years ago. He played a big part in that and felt pained. He fought back his own tears as she closed her eyes and turned her face away from him. "Serena, let's talk," he pleaded.

Serena shook her head, praying the tears and the pain would vanish behind her usual hard shell. "Malcolm, please I can't—" she swallowed over her tears. "Please, not now. Please."

He knew Serena—really knew her—and he knew for her to beg him for anything it had to mean a lot to her. Hating to release her from his arms, Malcolm reluctantly moved away from her and rose to pull on his pants. "Serena, I'm sorry—"

"I know."

He watched as she lay on her side, turning her back to him, and pulled the covers over her head. He sighed heavily as he reached for his clothes and got dressed. He grabbed a discarded blanket and lay down on the couch, glad that the fire had knocked the chill off the room. He wondered if there would ever be a repair for the chill lingering between him and Serena.

Chapter 7

"You . . . did . . . what!"

Serena regretted divulging the steamy moments Malcolm and she shared to Monique as soon as her friend shrieked like a banshee. Monique's look of pity was twice as bad. "Just a momentary lapse of good sense, nothing for you to have a stroke about," Serena said, trying to sound casual and light as she carefully steered her vehicle up the snow-covered Springfield Avenue toward Irvington.

Monique shifted in the passenger seat to look at Serena with a shake of her head. "What he do? Sneak in your bedroom last night? *Or* did you sneak into his?"

Serena stopped the car at a red light. "Nobody sneaked into anyone's room thankyouverymuch. And it didn't happen last night. This was two weeks ago. The night of the winter storm."

Monique raised a brow. "Don't be no man's fool, Serena," she warned. "If I was you, that man couldn't touch me with a ten-foot pole or a ten-foot anything else. See, I ain't no man's fool, especially one who . . ."

Serena tuned Monique *and* her self-glorifying rant out as she focused on her driving. Monique was always the one sistah in the bunch ranting and raving about what she's not putting up with from a man. And as always with those know-it-all militant sistahs, she was so busy digging all up and through everyone else's business that she missed—or ignored—the dirty drama in her own life.

"Humph. Where was all this I-am-woman crap when you took Tyrone back *after* you had to shave your privates as bald as Kojak 'cause he gave you crabs?" Serena said.

"Now that was low, Serena," Monique countered.

Serena stiffened, her face filling with dismay. "Did I say that out loud?"

"For your information I took Tyrone back because I wasn't sure if it was him or Daquan, my little stripper friend, that caused what I thought we agreed to refer to as 'the incident.' An incident we also agreed to never . . . ever . . . *ever* discuss again. Ever."

Serena remained silent.

"And don't forget I was there in those weeks after your marriage crumbled."

Yeah, you moved in and lived off me—rent free—for six months.

"I don't know why you agreed to live in that house with his no good, scandalous ass anyway," Monique griped, obviously wanting to have the last word . . . as always. "Now you're going to the wedding. Girl, what next?"

"Elaine's paying me to do the bridal party's hair, which is more than I can say for you, Miss-Forever-Looking-for-the-Hook-up."

"Hell, won't be too long for Malcolm to talk himself right into your drawers."

"Whatever, Monique," Serena muttered, but there was doubt lurking in the depths.

Truth be told the connection—that physical connection—between them was just as intense as it had been in the past. From the moment he touched her she was infused with a desire to be with him, around him . . . on him.

Your body feels so good, Serena.

Nearly two weeks later and Serena literally shivered from the memory of Malcolm's hot words breezing against her breasts. Problem was that she didn't want to remember how easily she gave in to his sexual charms and how close she came to blessing him with hers. She knew if he hadn't stuck his foot in his mouth and said the wrong thing—at the wrong time—that she would have let him make love to her right on that floor like all the bitterness between them never existed.

Your body is beautiful, Serena.

She pressed her thighs together to help ease the aching throb of her core. All these years later and Malcolm's touches and kisses made her lose her mind. *Damn him.*

"Shit me once . . . shame on you. Shit me twice . . . shame on me," Monique continued, as Serena pulled the vehicle into the crowded parking lot of a new mini-mall on Lyons Avenue. "You won't be happy 'til you're full up with Malcolm's thing."

And what a beautiful thing it is, Serena thought, an image of him nude by firelight causing her to flush with warmth.

"I'll tell you what," Serena offered, as she parked the car in a spot facing a salon with HAIR IT IS on the awning. "If we can lock away your . . . ahem, *incident,* then my near sexual excursion with my ex gets locked away too. Deal?"

Serena knew Monique didn't want to talk about how she had had more crabs than Red Lobster, so her friend's begrudging agreement was what she expected.

Serena didn't need anyone else to make her feel foolish or guilty. She was doing enough of that for herself. True, she let her head be overruled by desire but at least *the* deed had not been done. She found some solace in that.

Although she'd been tormented by sweaty nights dreaming of Malcolm's bald head pressed intimately between her thighs, Serena was determined not to let Malcolm get through her defenses.

For the past two weeks her ex-husband had made several attempts at finally having this big meaningful talk of his, but Serena had adamantly refused him the time of day. She came home from work as late as she could and went straight to her bedroom and locked the door.

Truth be told she was afraid.

Serena's soul was jumbled with emotions. Sadness over the dissolution of their marriage. Regret over the loss of their simplistic and innocent childhood friendship. Disappointment in herself for almost allowing Malcolm some nookie for "old times' sake." Frustration about having to keep living with Malcolm for an additional month to get the money she so desperately needed, but excitement—and a little fear— over finally owning and operating her own business.

It was amazing she wasn't sitting in the corner rocking and drooling while she dribbled her bottom lip.

Her "My Boo" ring tone sounded on her cell phone and her eyes darted down to where it sat on the top of her purse on the console. She released a harsh breath and rolled her eyes at the sight of Zander's name and home phone number on the Caller ID. "That's a sickening behind man," she muttered, annoyed that after all these weeks he was still trying for the impossible. She even thought she saw his car pass by the salon.

"Who?" Monique asked, leaning over to look down at the cell phone. "Oh, the mama's boy. Watch this."

Monique snatched up the cell phone and flipped it open before Serena could stop her.

"Hello."

Monique leaned back from Serena when she reached for the phone. "This *is* Serena. I just have a little cold."

Monique's smile was wicked as she winked at Serena.

"Uh-huh. No. Really? Wow."

Serena couldn't help but wonder what the hell Zander was saying that had Monique so intrigued.

"Listen, you're right, we do have a lot to talk about—"

Serena immediately released one hand from the steering wheel to futilely grab for her cell phone.

"Meet me at Mahogany's tonight at eight. Gotta go. Bye," Monique rushed before slamming the phone closed and dropping it back in Serena's purse.

"Why in the hell would you make a date for me with Zander?" Serena shrieked.

Monique just laughed and waved her hand as she began to search through her purse. "Chile please, his behind will sit there long enough, realize that your not gonna show and be so pissed that you stood him up that he won't call you anymore. He'll go home and cry in his mamma's big ole lap."

Serena looked doubtful.

"Trust me girl, it'll work," Monique said with way too much confidence.

"Girl, you got issues," Serena said, shaking her head.

Monique pulled air between her teeth. "You got an ex-boyfriend damn near stalking you and an ex-husband trying to get his freak on and you say *I* got issues. Please."

Serena focused her eyes on the empty salon sitting

before her very eager eyes. Eighteen hundred square feet of her dreams.

A short, portly man with skin the color of midnight stepped out of the door.

"That must be the realtor," Serena said to Monique, slipping on her gloves as she climbed out of her car.

Serena thought she heard Monique mutter, "Whoopdie do", but she didn't give it a second thought. All she wanted to do was see the inside of the salon.

The owner of Hair It Is was moving her business to New York to a more upscale location and listed the property for someone looking to take over the lease. The locale was great with plenty of foot traffic, bus service was right at the corner, and there was plenty of parking. Leasing was more advantageous to her than trying to buy her own commercial building—less headaches and worries being a renter than an owner. And the lease included all of the furnishings—which Serena hoped were in great working order. She was amped to check out the building.

"Hello, Mr. Steady." Serena smiled at the man, who only stood as tall as her chin, as she and Monique walked through the glass door the man held open for them.

Serena focused her attention on her surroundings. It was Sunday, so the salon was closed and she was able to see it all. She didn't exactly love the primary color scheme, but she loved the set-up of the salon. *Thank God the equipment is all black*, she thought, as she slowly walked to the back. There was even a small area upstairs being used for storage where Serena visualized a massage area.

Although it was much larger than she ever planned on—with a larger lease payment to match; although it was not in the booming downtown Newark area she wanted; although she knew she would have to revise her business plan and really start head-hunting for beauticians to rent the other booths, Serena wanted *this* place.

"This is perfect," Serena sighed with pleasure, sitting down in one of the unisex styling chairs.

Monique frowned up her nose as she looked around. "It's all right," she said.

Mr. Steady looked long and hard at Monique over the rim of his glasses, before he turned to Serena with his winning commission smile. "Well, I think this is a fabulous opportunity for you, Ms. Saint James—"

"Surprise, surprise," Monique muttered with sarcasm.

"Monique," Serena snapped sharply in irritation.

"If you want him to try and weasel you into leasing this dump, that's your business, but I'll be in the car." Monique gave Mr. Steady a nasty once-over before strolling out of the door like she was Queen of the Nile.

"I'm sorry, Mr. Steady."

He shook his head. "Never apologize for someone's else mistake."

"Sometimes you do something for so long it becomes second nature," she said softly as she looked out the glass door at Monique agitatedly pointing to her watch and motioning for Serena to hurry up.

At that moment Serena felt like a crab was nipping at her ankles trying to pull her back down into the barrel.

The second to last thing Malcolm wanted to do was be rude, but the absolute last thing he wanted to do was wrap up the pre-production for the day on his documentary to join his father, future stepmother and stepsister for a "get to know you before the wedding" dinner. Thank God he had Darrien, his reliable New

York assistant of the past four years, to handle the minute details he didn't have time for. Details like scheduling tapings with several multi-platinum selling artists—some he would have to fly out with on various tours during the next three months.

So he closed his laptop where he was doing some research online and stood from his lounging position on the bed to stretch his tall, muscular frame. He glanced down at his watch. It was definitely time for the Saint James replay of the Sunday afternoon dinner like on *Soul Food.*

He wasn't even 100 percent sure his father was going to 1) show up for the wedding and 2) actually say "I do".

I'll have to see it to believe it.

Malcolm took a quick shower before changing into his favorite vintage jeans and a long-sleeved white tee. He sprayed on his cologne and smoothed some cocoa butter on his bald head. He pulled on his camel-leather jacket as he jogged down the stairs and out the door to head to Elaine's.

Malcolm was just pulling his SUV away from the house when Serena passed him driving her own vehicle. His heart hammered against the wall of his chest and his eyes watched her like a hawk in his rearview mirror until she was out his sight.

Ever since the night of the winter storm, Serena was avoiding him like the plague. In many ways her silence and avoidance were worse than her anger. It wasn't that he almost made love to Serena in a fashion that would make sure he was remembered and constantly compared to. Hell, he wanted to bury his head, his lips and *himself* so deeply between her heavenly thighs that his mouth watered. He wasn't looking for a renewed commitment, but he had to admit that a steamy romp with his sexually explosive ex would have been just fine by him.

No, a sexual escapade—and that's all it would've been was sex—was not the issue. Nor was the fact that Serena shut him down from getting a taste of her goodies.

What was nagging him and torturing him with guilt was the unmistakable look of pure pain and hurt he saw in her eyes that night. A pain and hurt he caused. It was much easier for him to deal with her anger than her pain.

Serena did not wear her feelings on her sleeve. Her anger, sarcasm and quick wit were her ready shield to being hurt.

But that night her eyes were the windows to her soul and in the depths he saw raw feelings she couldn't hide.

"Damn," he swore, striking the steering wheel with his fist as he pulled to a stop at a red light.

He wanted things between them to be better. He knew that the die-hard, together-forever friendship they had as children was a place they could never re-visit. Still, he would love to be able to hold a civil conversation with her—even make her laugh like he used to—without this wall of resentment and anger between them.

He had a lot to make up for, that he knew, but he also wanted Serena to understand that he had been hurt by their marriage—and their divorce—as well. The first night he spent in his new apartment alone he had craved Serena so badly that he had to make himself man-up and not cry over the woman he loved more than anything in the world.

Serena and he needed closure or the wounds would never heal.

She couldn't give him the time of day but he would *make* the time in her life to have the conversation that should've gone down all those years ago.

Sighing, Malcolm forced Serena, their talk, and a

rather erotic vision of her naked body sprawled before the fireplace, from his thoughts as he turned his SUV into the drive of Elaine's house behind his father's newest Ford pick-up.

As soon as he stepped out of his vehicle, the front door opened. The doorway filled with a presence and Malcolm's eyes shifted. It was pure male instinct to look the young woman up and down from head to toe with an appreciative eye. She was a beauty, maybe too beautiful if that was at all possible. Tall and shapely with skin the color of pale butter and short wavy hair that was shockingly blond, it was hard for her not to draw a man's initial attention.

So this is Miracle, he thought, as he climbed the stairs.

"How you doin'?" he asked with that urban inflection in his tone that was common for East Coast men.

She smiled at him, causing her feline eyes to slant further. "Much . . . *much* better now," she purred, boldly stepping forward to hug him close. "Nice to meet you future stepbrother."

Malcolm's body stiffened and he raised a brow sharply as she pressed the full length of her frame against every contour of his body. He was quite sure she now knew the exact imprint of his member. It certainly was not the greeting between a soon-to-be stepbrother and stepsister.

"Miracle!" Elaine called from inside.

The woman unraveled herself from his body slowly with a wink before stepping aside and waving him into the house.

Malcolm smiled at her weakly as he passed her, still put off by her rather *warm* greeting.

"Mm, mm, mm," came from behind him.

He flinched and his eyes widened into saucers as she boldly cupped his buttocks with each of her hands.

Malcolm whirled to stare at her in shock but

Miracle just winked at him and breezed past him to enter the house with a husky laugh.

"She might need to lay off the hair dye," he grumbled, stepping into the foyer and closing the front door behind himself. "Must've soaked through to her brain."

Malcolm was being put in a corner—or propositioned by a woman. Problem was it was the wrong place, wrong time, and wrong woman. He frowned as a bare size-six foot crawled its way up his leg to press intimately against his crotch. He cast a stern look across the table at Miracle, who just winked and smiled as she took an awfully long time to lick the mashed potatoes from her fork.

Malcolm jerked his chair back, putting himself an awkward distance from the table.

"Something wrong, son?" Luther asked from the other end of the table.

Malcolm shifted his deep set eyes from Miracle to his father, forcing away the frown he wanted to display. The woman was coming on stronger to him than the funk of a mad skunk. Although the pressure was on, she did it with an innocent look on her face and slyness that left her mother and his father clueless to her advances.

"I'm straight, Pops, just felt like a gnat or bug nipping at my neck," Malcolm said with a brief glance at sweetly smiling Miracle.

"In the fall, son?" Luther asked, his face puzzled.

"Yeah," Malcolm said, casting a brief but meaningful look at Miracle. "Go figure."

"How's everything going at the house with Serena?" Luther asked around a mouthful of Elaine's homemade mashed potatoes and gravy.

"Serena?" Miracle asked. "Is that the ex-wife?"

Malcolm leveled those piercing mocha eyes on her, his senses immediately alert. "Yes, Serena's my . . . ex-wife."

He frowned at the way he had swallowed over a lump to say "ex-wife."

"I would be pissed if my Grandma made me live with my ex—"

"Miracle!" Elaine snapped sharply, her eyes piercing her daughter.

"What?" Miracle asked innocently, shrugging in nonchalance.

Luther cleared his throat and Malcolm knew his father disapproved of Miracle's brashness.

Malcolm saw Elaine reach over and lightly caress her father's hand and he was amazed to see the furrow between his father's brows disappear. Luther then lifted her hand and kissed her fingertips in a comfortable, loving gesture.

"Everything all set for Saturday?" Malcolm asked.

Elaine's face immediately lit up. "The wedding coordinator we hired has worked wonders. Beautiful fall foliage and lots of candles. I can hardly wait," she finished with a soft smile at Luther.

"All I need is the preacher and my baby, and I'm good to go," Luther said, looking at Elaine with warm sincerity.

"I'm really excited for both of you," Miracle added, looking at her mother and Luther with an innocent doe-eyed expression even as she attempted to inch her foot up Malcolm's leg again.

Having had it up to his bald head with the woman, Malcolm dropped his fork and stood. "Elaine, the food was excellent—"

"You going son?" Luther asked, his disappointment obvious. "I thought we would watch some football in a little bit."

"Yeah, no need rushing home to an ex-wife who don't want you around anyway," Miracle piped in.

"Miracle, help me clear these dishes," Elaine said, her voice as frigid as her eyes as she rose and began taking plates.

"But I—"

"Now." Elaine shot her daughter a meaningful glare.

"Young lady, most people learn as a child that it's better to be seen than heard," Luther said, his annoyance evident as he pointed at Miracle.

Elaine's glare flung down to Luther and Malcolm smelled trouble—big time.

"Luther, are you insinuating that I didn't properly raise my child?" she asked, her voice low but the implications of her sudden anger at her future husband heavy.

Luther turned his head slowly to look up at Elaine. His left eye jumped and Malcolm thought, *Oh, no.*

"Her actions speak for themselves," he threw back, his tone just as low but twice as cold.

"Pops, I can hang around a little bit longer," Malcolm asserted, trying to calm the anger simmering between the love birds. "Let's go watch the game. Philly's playing."

"My child can speak when she wants to," Elaine snapped.

Luther rose. "She ought to speak about things that's her business. Then again the limb don't fall too far from the tree."

Elaine released the dishes and they went clattering down against the table. "Now what the hell is *that* supposed to mean Luther Saint James?"

"Maybe if you wasn't flapping your lips on that phone with your big-mouthed daughter she wouldn't know all my son's business to dip in."

Elaine's mouth fell open.

"Hey, don't yell at my mother," Miracle shouted, rising to walk around the table to stand behind her mother.

Elaine's bottom lip quivered before she turned and flew from the room with a wail.

"Damn," Luther swore in a harsh whisper, before glaring one last time at Miracle and then striding out of the room in the direction Elaine flew.

Miracle turned to go in that direction but Malcolm reached out his hand like a striking rattlesnake and grabbed her wrist. "Hold your horses, you little trouble maker," he told her.

She cut her eyes up at him with a mischievous glint. "How'd you know I like it rough, daddy?"

"I see you let all that blond dye fry your brain," he snarled, releasing her wrist.

"Are you calling me stupid?" she asked with indignation.

Malcolm nodded. "And silly, immature—"

Miracle's eyes flashed with anger. "You ain't all that for you to stand up here and call me names, you Spike Lee reject."

Malcolm shrugged. "I'm not going to stand here and argue with you like children," he said over his shoulder as he left the room.

"You just mad 'cause you can't have all this," she said, following behind him.

Malcolm stopped and turned to look down at her with an annoyed expression. "You're just mad because I don't want it."

Miracle let her hands roam over the curves of her body. "Negro please, you ain't never had a woman as fine as me. Especially your ugly behind ex-wife. Bow-wow . . . bow-wow."

"You wish you were half the woman Serena is or that you looked half as good as Serena does," he replied honestly as he turned and continued into the foyer. "Your personality makes you ugly. Ugly as hell as a matter of fact."

Miracle laughed in disbelief, turning to study her face in the mirror on the wall of the foyer. "Please," she said in a drawn out fashion.

Malcolm didn't spare her a second look before leaving the house.

Tired of lying, sitting, and then sleeping in her bed during every moment she spent in the house, Serena had gathered her folder and was sitting at the island in the center of the modest kitchen, her notes spread before her, the tip of her pen clamped between her teeth as she tried so hard to focus on the load of work still ahead of her to open her own salon. Unfortunately she was distracted by a vision of Malcolm's supple lips sucking deeply at her nipples like there was nothing else in the world he would rather do.

Serena shivered at the thought, nearly biting the cap of her pen in half.

The last thing she wanted to do was desire Malcolm again, but her head was outruled by her body. The man was gorgeous. Everything about him, including the small knick on his chin from when he flipped off his bike, combined to make him sexy, dark, alluring, tempting, and . . . damn distracting.

Sighing, as she pushed away an image of Malcolm's chest and arms in his T-shirt, Serena forced herself to focus on juggling what little money she had—or was going to have—so that she could afford what she now called her dream salon.

But . . .

His abs sure are nice though. Hell, better than Usher's!

"So you're out of your room."

Serena looked up at the words suddenly spoken in

the room and there Malcolm stood, like he just walked out of her thoughts. It was disconcerting.

Nervous under his piercing gaze, Serena stood and began gathering her things quickly . . . anxiously. "I'll be out of here in just a sec," she said, not looking at him at all even as the scent of his cologne wafted to tease her senses.

"Don't run on my account," Malcolm said, walking forward to reach out and grab her hand loosely.

Serena looked up out of instinct and their eyes locked. For one vulnerable moment, Serena allowed herself to get lost in the good times they once shared. The friendship, the loyalty, the passion, the mind-blowing sex . . . all of it gone in what now seemed like a heartbeat.

Serena broke their gaze first, easing her wrist out of his grasp. She felt relief *and* regret when he let her wrist go.

"Serena, I'm sorry that I hurt you all those years ago. Never ever would I do anything to cause you pain intentionally," he said in a quiet voice that spoke volumes just as she reached the kitchen's archway.

His words left her frozen in place.

"I want to put this behind us—"

"No," Serena said, shaking her head.

She heard his footsteps carry him closer and her body, her treacherous body, reacted to his nearness as her pulse raced and nipples hardened in a rush.

"We have ten years of friendship gone. A friendship I think we should have fought harder to keep. I miss my friend," he said, his words caressing the nape of her neck and his scent enfolding her body like his very arms.

Serena shivered.

"I miss laughing with you and talking to you and getting your advice. I miss seeing you smile at one of my corny jokes. I miss hanging out with you."

An Important Message From The ARABESQUE Publisher

Dear Arabesque Reader,

I invite you to join the club! The Arabesque book club delivers four novels each month right to your front door! It's easy, and you will never miss a romance by one of our award-winning authors!

With upcoming novels featuring strong, sexy women, and African-American heroes that are charming, loving and true... you won't want to miss a single release. Our authors fill each page with exceptional dialogue, exciting plot twists, and enough sizzling romance to keep you riveted until the satisfying end! To receive novels by bestselling authors such as Gwynne Forster, Janice Sims, Angela Winters and others, I encourage you to join now!

Read about the men we love... in the pages of Arabesque!

Linda Gill
PUBLISHER, ARABESQUE ROMANCE NOVELS

*P.S. Watch out for the next Summer Series **"Ports Of Call"** that will take you to the exotic locales of Venice, Fiji, the Caribbean and Ghana! You won't need a passport to travel, just collect all four novels to enjoy romance around the world! For more details, visit us at www.BET.com.*

A SPECIAL "THANK YOU" FROM ARABESQUE JUST FOR YOU!

Send this card back and you'll receive 4 FREE Arabesque Novels—
a $25.96 value—absolutely FREE!

The introductory 4 Arabesque Romance books are yours FREE
(plus $1.99 shipping & handling). If you wish to continue to
receive 4 books every month, do nothing. Each month, we will
send you 4 New Arabesque Romance Novels for your free exami-
nation. If you wish to keep them, pay just $18* (plus, $1.99 shipping & handling). If you decide not to continue, you owe nothing!

- Send no money now.
- Never an obligation.
- Books delivered to your door!

We hope that after receiving your FREE books you'll want to
remain an Arabesque subscriber, but the choice is yours! So why
not take advantage of this Arabesque offer, with no risk of any
kind. You'll be glad you did!

In fact, we're so sure you will love your Arabesque novels, that
we will send you an Arabesque Tote Bag FREE with your first
paid shipment.

* PRICES SUBJECT TO CHANGE.

YOU'LL GET
4 SELECT
ROMANCES PLUS
THIS FABULOUS
TOTE BAG!

ARABESQUE

**Visit us at:
www.BET.com**

THE "THANK YOU" GIFT INCLUDES:

- 4 books absolutely FREE (plus $1.99 for shipping and handling).
- A FREE newsletter, *Arabesque Romance News*, filled with author interviews, book previews, special offers, and more!
- No risks or obligations. You're free to cancel whenever you wish with no questions asked.

INTRODUCTORY OFFER CERTIFICATE

Yes! Please send me 4 FREE Arabesque novels (plus $1.99 for shipping & handling). I understand I am under no obligation to purchase any books, as explained on the back of this card. Send my free tote bag after my first regular paid shipment.

NAME _____

ADDRESS _____ APT. ____

CITY _____ STATE _____ ZIP _____

TELEPHONE ( ) _____

E-MAIL _____

SIGNATURE _____

Offer limited to one per household and **not** valid to current subscribers. All orders subject to approval. Terms, offer, & price subject to change. Tote bags available while supplies last.

Thank You!

AN125A

ARABESQUE

Accepting the four introductory books for FREE (plus $1.99 to offset the cost of shipping & handling) places you under no obligation to buy anything. You may keep the books and return the shipping statement marked "cancelled". If you do not cancel, about a month later we will send 4 additional Arabesque novels, and you will be billed the preferred subscriber's price of just $4.50 per title. That's $18.00* for all 4 books for a savings of almost 30% off the cover price (Plus $1.99 for shipping and handling). You may cancel at any time, but if you choose to continue, every month we'll send you 4 more books, which you may either purchase at the preferred discount price. . . or return to us and cancel your subscription.

THE ARABESQUE ROMANCE CLUB: HERE'S HOW IT WORKS

THE ARABESQUE ROMANCE BOOK CLUB
P.O. BOX 5214
CLIFTON NJ 07015-5214

PLACE
STAMP
HERE

Serena closed her eyes tightly, grimacing in sweet agony as she released a breath heavy with emotions that threatened to spill from her trembling lips.

"If I could just turn back the hands of time I would have you back in my life as the best friend I ever had," he said with conviction.

Serena felt pain clutch her heart at his words. She turned slowly, her folded arms brushing his body from their closeness and she opened her eyes and felt drowned in the mocha depths of his eyes. "I was a better friend than wife, huh?" she asked softly.

Malcolm smiled just a little.

"That's just what a woman wants to hear from a man."

Malcolm's smile fell like a ton of bricks.

Serena turn and fled up the stairs before he could even blink or think. She closed the door of the bedroom and locked it securely behind her. She heard Malcolm's heavy footsteps hit each step as he ran upstairs.

She tensed as the steps stopped at her door.

"Serena, that's not how I meant that," he said through the door, his words muffled through the solid wood.

She said nothing.

"Serena," Malcolm called out again.

She didn't relax her body again until the footsteps carried him away from her door.

Zander popped the collar of his favorite striped button-up shirt as he stepped out of his car in the parking lot of Mahogany's and pulled on his leather jacket. The soft refrains of jazz music reached him outside as he briskly walked through the cold night to the club's entrance.

He wasn't sure what he expected from tonight.

After weeks of begging and pleading, Serena had finally agreed to see him. His ego wouldn't let him let her go that easy. What woman wouldn't want him? What woman would leave him for another man—especially with the shortage of fine, upstanding brothers like himself these days. Educated, employed, drug free, criminal-record free. Hell, he knew he was the cream of the crop.

A lot of this was about proving to himself that he could—and would—have Serena back. Hadn't his mama always raised him to believe that *he* was special, that any woman would be lucky to have him?

"Welcome to Mahogany's."

Zander smiled at the sight of the beautiful owner of the restaurant/jazz club, Mahogany Woods. "Thank you. How are you doing this evening?" he asked, his eyes warmly appreciating her physical attributes.

"I'm blessed and I wish you many blessings as well," she said with her usual open and friendly demeanor. "Dining alone?"

"I'm meeting Serena Saint James for dinner."

Mahogany nodded. "She's awaiting you. Right this way."

Zander followed Mahogany, his eyes skimming the faces of the diners over her slender shoulders. He didn't see Serena. *Maybe she has a table upstairs?*

Zander did see Serena's wild and crazy best friend Monique at a table and he waved to her in what he thought was passing until Mahogany came to a stop at her table.

"You two enjoy your dinner. Your waitress will be right with you," Mahogany said before taking her leave with a smile.

Zander remained standing, his face confused as he looked down at Monique's face. "Why did Serena invite you to dinner with us?" he asked with obvious annoyance.

"Boy, sit down," Monique said lightly.

Zander took his seat.

"Serena's not here," Monique said as soon as he sat.

Zander stood up like a spring was in his seat.

"She sent me to get it through to you that things were over between the two of you, a'ight."

Zander frowned, feeling like a fool. "Now ain't this some shit."

Monique pouted and looked at him sadly. "Yes, ain't it?"

Chapter 8

"Sure you don't want to go to Elaine's for Thanksgiving dinner?" Malcolm asked a few days later when he and Serena crossed paths in the kitchen.

Serena took a long sip of her hot chocolate. "I'm having dinner at Monique's," she lied, moving out of the kitchen.

"Serena, about what I said the other day. I—"

"What, Malcolm? What?" she snapped, whirling on him.

"You know what, your attitude is disgusting," he said, picking his coat from where he sat it atop the island.

Serena turned back around to leave the room. "Yeah well so is your breath," she threw over her shoulder.

"Grow up, Serena."

"Grow some hair, Kojak."

"This from the weave queen."

"Make an appointment I'll hook you up too."

"Serena," he called out softly.

She turned to look at him, her eyes annoyed.

"Happy Thanksgiving," was all that he said.

"Thanks. You too," she answered begrudgingly, before continuing out of the kitchen.

Seconds later the sound of the kitchen door closing echoed through the house as Serena made her way to the den for a day of T & R—television and relaxation.

She had no intention of another ghetto-fabulous holiday at Monique's with her canned and boxed food— and that was everything from the ham to the dinner rolls. On top of that, Serena wasn't particularly fond of Monique's big-mouthed club buddies and the last thing she wanted to do was spend her day listening to stories from their drama-filled lives.

So she stretched out on the floor, turned the television to one of those corny parades and tried her best not to reminisce too hard on how good her Auntie's cornbread dressing would be right about then. She succeeded for about an hour before her stomach started to rumble loudly in protest.

Serena made her way to the kitchen and stood before the refrigerator trying her best to form a taste for what it had to offer . . . and failed. She wanted dressing the way an addict wanted her drug.

Feeling motivated, Serena walked over to the pantry and began pulling out all the necessary ingredients to make her own dinner. "Why the hell not?" she said to herself.

She made a list of what little ingredients she was missing. "Nothing a little trip to Pathmark can't take care of," she said, as she jogged upstairs to grab her coat, purse, and keys.

"Miracle sure does talk too much," Luther said in low tones to Malcolm as he and Malcolm sipped on cold beers and tried to enjoy the football game with the rest of Elaine's family assembled in her den.

"Uh, huh."

Malcolm let his eyes drift to the blonde as she sat on the arm of the chair quizzing a male cousin on the ins and outs of football.

"Elaine thinks that girl's poop don't stink," Luther grumbled behind his can.

"Uh-huh."

Malcolm tried to focus on the game, leaning forward as the running back made a dash for the end zone.

"She gets on my nerves," Luther added.

Malcolm raised his can in toast to that one.

"She needs a *good* behind cutting."

"Want my belt?" Malcolm offered, beginning to wonder just what Miracle had done to tick his father— generally a good-natured man—off so much.

Miracle rose and walked in front of the television. Everyone in the room, including Malcolm, hollered for her to move out of the way.

Everyone except Luther, who muttered, "Sit *down* some where."

Malcolm rose and stepped over his father's outstretched legs to leave the room and head to the bathroom in the hall. He shut the door behind himself and sighed as he relieved himself. After washing his hands and checking out his profile in the mirror, Malcolm opened the door and ran smack dead into Miracle lounging against the door frame.

"Sorry 'bout that," he said, shifting to the right to walk past her.

Miracle shifted as well.

Releasing a breath that spoke volumes of his irritation, Malcolm looked down at her. "Can I help you with something, Miracle?"

"More like *I* can help *you*."

Malcolm started to step back but realized she could— and probably would—trap him in the bathroom.

"Doubt that," he said, using his hands to pick her up and set her out of his path.

He made his way back to the den, reclaiming his seat by his father. Miracle made him nervous. She was like a crackhead trying to use her wares for a hit. She was fanatical about coming onto him and he would be more than glad to see the last of her after the wedding.

She came back into the den and squeezed on the sofa beside him.

His father and Mama James had raised him to be a gentleman, but he had the distinct feeling he was going to have to cuss Miracle out before she left him alone.

Elaine came to stand at the doorway of the den, wiping her hands on a dish towel. "Who's winning?"

"Eagles," Luther answered, looking up at his fiancé with a soft smile.

"I think they should change their name to Philadelphia Emeralds because their uniforms are so green," Miracle added. "Isn't that nicer than *eagles?*"

Luther's smile dropped.

"When that food gone be ready, Lainey?" her Uncle Fritz asked from his spot in the corner.

"Now Uncle Fritz you know we have dinner at six P.M. every year and nothing's changed this year."

"Six!" Luther and Malcolm exclaimed together. Comically they both also looked down at their watches.

It was just two o'clock.

Man, no way in hell, Malcolm thought as Miracle whispered in his ear about how flexible she was.

Malcolm rose to his feet.

"Where you going, son?" Luther asked.

"Just finishing up my rounds at a couple of friend's houses, gather a few takeout plates, and then take them to the house," he said. "I might swing back through later on."

"I'll make you a plate and bring it to the rehearsal tomorrow," Elaine offered as Malcolm bent down to kiss her smooth cheeks.

Malcolm ignored the alluring looks Miracle was shooting his way as he said his good-byes and walked out of the house. He hated to admit that he'd rushed into his SUV and pulled away from the curb before Miracle could gather enough steam to catch up to him.

Hell, he knew he was a good looking man, but he couldn't for the life of him sniff out just what her motivation was in coming on so strong.

Deciding it wasn't worth any further thought, Malcolm used his remote to play his John Legend CD. As John sung the hell out of "Ordinary People" Malcolm was going over in his head some new concepts he was thinking of for the documentary. It would mean revising pre-production but he wanted it to have an edgier feel and the lighting effects to be more graphic and artistic.

He didn't even realize that he was sitting at a light adjacent to the cemetery where Mama James was buried until he looked over to his left.

Damn.

When the light turned green he made the left turn to take him inside the burial ground and easily made his way to the area where she was buried.

As he parked the car and stepped down out of his vehicle, he saw that many of the headstones were covered with fresh and artificial floral arrangements. There were several clusters of people standing around plots throughout the area.

He wished he'd brought flowers. Maybe bunches of the lavender she cherished so much. As he stood next to the double plot of Mama and Papa James, his eyes were fixed on their elaborately carved headstone. "At least they're together now," he said to the wind, his only companion as he fought not to let his tears free.

He didn't talk to her because he knew that his grandmother could hear him anytime and anywhere but he squatted next to the plot and thought of her. Enjoyed the good memories of her. Cherished the love she gave him freely and respected the manner in which she raised him.

And then he thought of her insistence on seeing Serena and him reunite. He never could deny that Mama James was one of the wisest souls he ever encountered, but her die-hard belief in Serena and him rediscovering love was more romanticism than common sense.

Their time had come and gone. Now it was about finishing their task so that he could have the house free and clear and Serena could have her own business. That's all there was to it for both of them.

Malcolm thought of his ex-wife.

Sure she was more mature, even more beautiful and vibrant, more patient, a *little* less filled with animosity, more focused and determined . . . but some other things remained like her friendship with a nut like Monique. They had nothing in common and he failed to see, even now, why they remained friends.

Years ago he used to blame Monique for the end of his marriage. Her influence on Serena had hurt them but in the end Serena knew she was a married woman and thus her lifestyle could not be the same as her live-life-to-the-fullest fiend.

No, as much as Monique continued to annoy him, Serena was ultimately responsible for her own actions, just like he was responsible for his own.

Yes, he'd had a short temper with his young wife. Yes, he had wanted things done his way or no way. Yes, he had pushed her away with his rules of what was wrong and right for a bride—*his* bride.

And then of course what he did to her had been the ultimate act of a young fool. He had no one to blame but himself for the anger Serena still carried for him.

They both could have handled things differently.

Sighing heavily, Malcolm rose easily and made his way back to his vehicle. Maybe, just maybe if they had handled things differently Serena and he would still be married, with a houseful of babies and even more dreams.

He admitted to himself that the concept of that didn't sound bad at all.

Serena remembered the first time she cooked Thanksgiving dinner. The cornbread had been fresh—unseasoned. The bird had been cold and bloody at the bone. The macaroni and cheese salty. She had only been sixteen and had begged Auntie to let her make the dinner that year.

Unfortunately, Auntie had agreed.

She invited Malcolm to share in her first feast and really wanted things to be good to impress who she knew would be her husband one day.

Serena had cleared her aunt out of the kitchen, positive that her years of watching and assisting Auntie made her more than qualified to handle things by herself.

How wrong she was.

Serena actually laughed as she remembered the look on Auntie and Malcolm's face as they first eagerly dug into the meal that *looked* great.

Needless to say they all hustled over to Mama James' for dinner after chugging down lots of bottled fruit punch to kill the taste of the food.

"Well check me out now," Serena joked to herself as she pulled the stuffing out of the oven with mitts.

Sitting the small dish on the island, Serena surveyed her feast. Two baked Cornish hens, macaroni and cheese, cornbread stuffing, potato salad, collard greens with ham hocks, and candied yams.

"Serena?" Malcolm walked into the kitchen and closed the door behind himself.

Serena was startled by his sudden appearance . . . again. Her hand flew up to flatten any stray hairs back into her ponytail. "I thought you were going to Elaine's."

Malcolm smiled and her heart double pumped. "I thought you were going to Monique's," he countered, coming to take in the sights and smells of her feast for one. "I'm not interrupting anything, am I?"

"No, no," Serena said. "I decided to pass on Monique's and just cooked a little something for myself."

"You always did love dressing," he mused. "Remember your first Thanksgiving dinner?"

Serena smiled and laughed softly. "I was *just* thinking about that actually. You had to give me an 'A' for effort."

"It wasn't that . . . bad," he offered with a smile that made his eyes twinkle mischievously.

Malcolm's stomach grumbled loudly and he looked bashful. "What?" he asked, as Serena raised a brow. "A brotha hungry, shoot."

"How do you know it doesn't taste as bad as it did that first time?" Serena teased, actually feeling comfortable around him again.

"I doubt that, you've seemed to have gotten better at a lot of things," he said, as he shrugged out of his jacket.

He looked over at Serena who just avoided his gaze.

Serena washed her hands and reached for two

plates out of the cabinet. "Have some," she offered, handing him a plate. "I'll share my feast with you."

Malcolm accepted the plate. "Willing to share your company as well?" he asked in a deeply masculine tone.

Serena shot him a don't-even-play-yourself look.

"Come on, it's the holidays and it's just dinner, Serena," he protested as he fixed his plate.

To be honest, Serena didn't want to eat alone. "Whatever," she said, very blasé.

Malcolm just smiled, pleased for the chance to subtly make things better between them. "Would be nice to eat in the dining room."

Too cozy, Serena thought, shaking her head. "Den."

"Deal."

They fixed their food in silence and carried their plates and glasses of lemonade into the den, both settling on the floor at either ends of the coffee table.

Malcolm raised his glass and reached toward Serena. "Here's to Mama and Papa James and Auntie, who are all probably enjoying the holiday together. To our family and friends—except Monique—"

"Malcolm," Serena chastised with a slight scowl.

"Okay, Monique too," he added begrudgingly. "And here's to old friends becoming new friends again."

Serena snorted in a very unladylike fashion, not paying his words of them being best buds again any attention before she dug into her food. And it tasted pretty good.

"How's the search coming for a salon?" Malcolm asked.

Serena nodded. "I found a place that I really like. Just working all the details."

"I'm happy for you, Serena."

Serena looked up at the sincerity in his deep, timbered tone. "Thank you. I'm happy for me, too. I really want this to be successful and I'm willing to put in the work to make it happen, you know?"

"That's the determined Serena I remember growing up with," Malcolm said, his smile crinkling the corners of his eyes. "Whatever you set your mind to do you got it done."

"Even if it got us in trouble sometimes."

"Yeah, like the time you were on punishment because of the failing grade in art of all things—"

Serena's eyes widened. "That hag Mrs. Barnum hated me and the feeling was mutual."

"Yeah, but Auntie said you couldn't go to the basketball game and you snuck out anyway." Malcolm laughed as he remembered Serena trying to sneak back into the house after they successfully snuck her out to make the game.

"Auntie was a trip. She was sitting in the middle of my bed when I got back into my room . . . with a belt."

"Got me in trouble too. Mama James said I was your accomplice."

"That was a good game though," Serena laughed.

"Yeah, the team won the division championship."

"Humph, couldn't sit down for a few hours but it was worth it."

"Remember when we hit my father's signed Reggie Jackson baseball over the park wall?" Malcolm asked.

"Do I remember? I had a nervous stomach for the next two weeks scared he would find out."

They reminisced over other moments they shared as friends, both steering clear of the years where they made the fatal step over the line from friends to lovers. The conversation remained on neutral topics: the clothes they used to wear, the hairstyles they should have been ashamed to sport, the trouble they got into and the time they got away with dirt.

After a while they fell into comfortable silence with Serena full and slumped back against the sofa.

She felt Malcolm's eyes on hers and held up her hand before he even began.

"No, no, no. All I'm asking for is a truce while we're here. No arguing. No insulting. No drama. No heated kisses in front of fireplaces . . . ," Malcom entreated.

She looked over and their eyes locked. Memories of that steamy night and the many nights they shared in the past played in their eyes like a movie.

Don't let him off that easy, her mind said.

Malcolm was admittedly a very handsome man with his rugged, dark appeal. There was wildness about him that made you curious as to the mystery in his eyes and as to what would make him smile—something he rarely seemed to do. He was appealing, but it was more than his mysterious good looks with his high brow, defined cheeks and lips so divinely soft that you longed to suckle and feast upon them. And more than his style that was seventy-five percent urban sophistication and twenty-five percent rugged thuggishness in a white tee and Timbs. And more than his cool confidence. His b-boy swagger. Divine sexiness. Intelligence. Raw energy. His intensity. It was all of these things and more.

Like the body hidden beneath his baggy clothes. Be it draped in silk or cotton, every muscle and sculptured contour of Malcolm's body was a testament to his physical fitness. Arms of steel. Chest rock solid. Abs to bounce a quarter on. Thighs that seemed strong enough to support the weight of the world.

And of course there was his sex. Thick and throbbing even at rest, it always seemed to be one pulse away from complete, fulfilling hardness.

Umph . . . umph . . . umph.

Yes, the brother was bad and there was no denying that.

But . . .

He had broken her heart into a thousand pieces and she *had* to remember that. "I'm going to get a beer, want one?" she offered, rising to move out of the room before he could even answer.

She wanted—needed—to get the hell away from Malcolm, his memories, and his magnetism.

Something in him—about him—had always called to her, drawing her into him since the first day they met and she didn't want to succumb to *it* again.

Look what happened the last time, she warned herself darkly as she grabbed two Heinekens from the fridge. *Get it together. This is Malcolm. My ex-husband. And no matter how good he's looking and smelling—sweet Jesus— this man hurt me like nothing before ever did or ever will.*

"Turn on the game, Saint James," Serena said as she entered the room. She held out his beer to him, being sure to avoid that inevitable jolt of electricity by avoiding contact with his hand.

"That'll work," Malcolm said, obviously dropping his let's-be-friends-speech . . . for now.

"Philly's playing and I love me some deliciously thick Donovan McNabb."

Malcolm felt pure jealousy course through his veins. One slashing brow rose in mocking. "He ain't got nothing on me but a great throwing arm," he muttered, just a bit darkly as he turned the television to the game already in progress.

Serena paused with her beer just at her open lips, turning her head to look at him like he was on something. "Negro, *please*," she drawled with a laugh that echoed into her bottle.

"Bet *he* can't make you hum."

Serena flushed with warmth and remembrance, but she hid her feelings from Malcolm's all-too-knowing eyes. When she was deep into the throes of a climax, she would emit a long, delicious, drawn out hum that had the distinct sound of bees buzzing around honey.

Malcolm's main ambition had been making her hum . . . and he had been so good at it. *Didn't do so bad the night of the winter storm either,* she mused, with a slight quiver of her core.

At his smug look, Serena leaned her head back against the couch, let her eyes drift close, and began to imitate that very humming noise that let him know she was being pleased. This was in true mischievous Serena fashion.

"Hmmmmmm," she started with a light purr.

A shot of pure heat radiated from the tip of his size-thirteen feet to the tip of his member with a jolt.

Serena licked her lips slowly and kicked it up a notch more than Emeril ever could. "Hmmmmmm-mmmmmmmmmmmmmmmmmmmmm."

Malcolm was glad her eyes were closed as his sex swelled to a stiffness to rival an iron pole. Her noises sounded way too similar to the real humming she used to do when he was buried deep within her stroking like his life depended on it.

His hands itched to spank her butt.

His mouth wanted to kiss her.

His member wanted to get lost inside of her walls.

"Oh, trust me, you weren't faking it," he said with confidence.

Serena opened one eye to look at him. "Don't be so sure," she teased.

Malcolm stretched his legs out in front of him and adjusted his thankfully baggy cords, allowing his aching stiffness more room to breathe and stretch as he awaited for his arousal to ease.

He wanted to say: "You can't fake wetness or the feel of your walls clutching me as you came," but he didn't.

Again they were treading on dangerous ground.

Entering a zone where their desire overruled their heads. The electricity between them was undeniable.

Serena leaned forward, through with her game as she reached for her beer with a sidelong glance at him. "At least I didn't st-st-st-st-stutter," she mumbled with a soft and-what smile.

Malcolm stared at his ex-wife long and hard as she barely contained her laughter at his expense. "I didn't stutter," he insisted in a deeply masculine voice that was heavy with his East Coast attitude.

"Yeah, okay . . . sure you d-d-d-d-d-didn't," she said, ending with a shriek of laughter as she clutched her chest and kicked her feet.

Malcolm just shook his head at her. *Same old, Ree,* he thought, and realized that wasn't a bad thing. Serena had always been the fun-loving one, free with her outrageous and infectious laughter. In the good days of Serena & Malcolm, she had made him want to laugh and have fun like no else could.

He missed that about her. Just like if he was honest with himself he knew he missed the scent of her perfume clinging faintly to the sheets. Or the feel of her warm breasts and thighs pressed intimately against the back of him as they slept. Or the way she would straddle his strong back and give him actual goose bumps from the very feel of her hands as she stroked his back and buttocks with ease. Or the feel of her gloriously full lips as she kissed, suckled, and tasted his neck, his nipples, his abs and his member until he felt weak and lightheaded.

Serena had always been the type of woman most men craved: a lady in the street, a buddy about sports events, and a woman offering total sexual satisfaction in bed. A triple threat.

"There's McNabb and look how nicely his behind fills out that uniform. Whoo!" Serena bounced up and down on the floor excitedly.

Malcolm felt the tightening of his stomach muscles, amazed at the jealousy he felt. "Looks like he could use some time on the Stairmaster to me," he muttered darkly, pointedly raising the remote to turn up the volume and drown out her one-woman cheering squad for the quarterback. At that moment he wished he was on the opposing team so that he could tackle the man *he* dubbed one of the all around best QBs in the game.

"Atlanta gone crush 'em," he said, although he thought differently. He just wanted to egg her on and Serena took the bait.

Her competitive spirit kicked into overdrive. "Sounds like the makings of a bet to me," she said, looking at him and then looking away as she felt breathless from the intensity of his eyes. *Handsome devil.*

"Bet then," he said, flashing her a charming smile that crinkled the corners of his eyes and illuminated his face.

Serena kicked off the flip-flops she was wearing as house shoes and folded her legs Indian style.

Malcolm tried not to notice the way the plump lips of her core now pressed against the seat of her pants.

"When Philly wins, you cook dinner for me all next week."

"And when Atlanta wins?" he asked, picking up his plate to scrape the last of the stuffing up onto his fork.

"Choice is yours."

Malcolm pondered just what he wanted from her, not wanting to pass up the opportunity *if* his team actually lost. Deciding to keep it PG, "I want what I couldn't have on the regular when we weren't married."

Serena's eyes dropped below his belt.

"Get your mind out of the gutter," Malcolm told her, glad his erection had eased.

"What was I thinking? You got that more than enough."

Malcolm's grin widened and he dropped his head as he used his hand to unsuccessfully wipe the grin from his face. "True, true."

Serena shot him a withering look.

Malcolm licked his lips and feigned a serious expression. "You have to do whatever I say for one week."

Serena snorted in her very unladylike fashion. "Nothing doing. I can just see me butt naked with nothing but a frown serving you peeled grapes or something stupid along those lines."

Malcolm couldn't help but picture that and his grin widened further until it resembled that of a Cheshire cat.

Serena picked up a throw pillow and hit him in the face with it.

"Okay, fine. Atlanta wins and you dance with me at the reception Saturday."

Serena looked doubtful. "That's it?"

Malcolm nodded. "That's it. Bet?"

"Bet."

Chapter 9

"Thanks, but no thanks. I don't let amateurs in my head."

Serena's jaw clenched at the very sound of Miracle's voice and she had the distinct desire to knock the wind out of the woman. They were at Hair Happenings as Serena worked all morning to complete the hair for Elaine and her entire bridal party—luckily it was just three of her friends and her daughter. One by one the women had come in for their appointments starting at eight that morning. Her last clients for the day were Elaine and Miracle. Pointedly, she looked at Miracle's harshly bleached hair. "Too late for that, don't you think?"

Some of the ladies in the salon snickered. One laughed outright. All of them had picked up on Miracle's attitude.

"I'm used to being hated for the way I look," she told Serena simply with a shrug.

"Oh no, she didn't!"

"Cocoa Barbie needs to sit her silly self down somewhere!"

The comments from the women in the salon floated into the air, but Miracle didn't blink.

Serena knew then that the girl was touched—as Auntie used to put it about crazy people.

Serena frowned and paused in gathering up her supplies to look at the woman over her shoulder. "Listen, if you don't want your hair done that's fine. Why are you here?" Serena asked, deciding to take the high road because she was much older than the childish woman seeking attention in all the wrong ways.

"Wanted to see Mal's ex," she said.

The immediate area of the salon around Serena went quiet and she was aware of twenty pairs of eyes on them. Drama was meant for the soap operas and romance novels, not her life . . . not anymore anyway. Serena released a bored sigh, even though she felt gut punched. Was Malcolm messing around with this . . . this mental child?

You know what, I don't even care.

Serena refused to admit to the jealousy she felt. "What do you want, Miracle?" Serena asked with patience that was fading fast.

"I can't imagine you two together."

Serena's eyes twitched and she knew if this woman kept pushing her buttons that she would no longer be able to contain her temper. In her twenties she would've twisted her fingers into what little hair Miracle had on her head and then rammed her face into a toilet bowl.

Ah, the patience of thirties.

"I'm going to be in one of his videos," she said with pride.

Serena raised a brow. "His *videos?*" she asked with obvious confusion.

"I think you can see that I am meant to be a video vixen," Miracle said, actually turning. "I look just as good as that girl in the Usher video."

Serena burst out laughing at the girl's foolish-ness. "You think Malcolm does music videos?"

Miracle's smile fell just a bit. "What's so funny?"

"Not only does Malcolm *not* do music videos, sweetheart, he would be a little insulted if you even told him that."

Miracle's smile was completely gone. "But my mother said she watched one of his videos."

"No, Malcolm does documentaries . . . not music videos."

Miracle's disappointment was obvious.

"Is that what you were sniffing up on?" Serena asked in a feigned disappointed voice. "Aw poor baby, you wanted to let Nelly slide a credit card down the crack of your butt too?"

The women in the salon all burst out laughing.

"Ya'll are just jealous," Miracle said spitefully, grabbing her purse and walking out of the salon with her conceited head held ever so high.

Elaine walked up to them, returning from the restroom, with wallet in hand. Her hair was ele-gantly styled in an updo and her makeup was natu-ral and fresh looking—all thanks to Serena. The blushing bride looked as beautiful as she should on her wedding day.

"Where's Miracle?" Elaine asked as she began to write a check.

The ladies bust out laughing again and Serena could only bite the inside of her cheek to keep from doing so. "She's waiting outside."

Elaine tore the check out to hand to Serena, look-ing out the window at Miracle talking animatedly on her cell phone. "Still coming to the wedding aren't you?" she asked with a soft smile.

"Yes. As a matter of fact I'm done for the day and I'm heading home to do something with my own head. Everything okay, Elaine?" Serena asked with concern as the older woman bit off her lipstick.

"I haven't heard from Luther all morning," she admitted in a whispered rush, her eyes filled with panic.

"I'm sure everything's fine," Serena assured her, although she wouldn't doubt it if old Luther wasn't halfway to the state line by now.

"You know, you're right. It's just nerves," Elaine said, with a smile that didn't quite reach her eyes.

Serena watched the woman leave the salon, thinking heavily of Luther's track record with weddings. She hoped for Elaine's sake that he had the balls to follow through this time.

"I'm not doing it, son, and there's nothing you can say to change my mind!"

Malcolm could strangle his father *if* he didn't have the respect and the good sense not to. One hour before his wedding and Luther was sitting in his apartment, dressed in a track suit, drinking a lite beer and watching a Rocky marathon on television.

When his father didn't arrive at the house at noon as they planned, Malcolm started to get a *little* nervous. When he tried calling his father and couldn't get an answer on his cell or his home phone, Malcolm's stomach got the bubble guts. He drove over to his father's apartment to find the man adamantly refusing to show up for yet another wedding he agreed to.

Malcolm loosened the bow tie, already dressed in his tuxedo, as he came to squat down next to his father sitting in his favorite recliner. A recliner he had yet to move into Elaine's house because he refused to watch TV without it.

"Pops, I don't mean any disrespect because you and Mama James always raised me to have that respect for you or for anyone that was my elder," Malcolm began in low dulcet tones like he was talking someone off a ledge. "I've been watching you play these games with women for years and I'm lucky that I never let it change the type of man I am and how I feel about marriage and women."

Luther frowned.

"Elaine is a beautiful person and she loves you and you love her, but why did you propose if you weren't going through with it? Why *aren't* you going through with it? And . . . and . . . what's *wrong* with you, man?" he finished in exasperation.

"I loved your mother, son. I still love her," Luther began with a voice raw with emotion.

"But Pops—"

"No, let me finish. You asked me, now let me answer you."

Malcolm moved to take a seat on the sofa adjacent to his father.

"You never really knew her. She was beautiful and sweet, but boy she wouldn't take no stuff off me, you know?" Luther smiled with his memories. "I knew that when I met her that I would never love another woman the same way again and when I lost her . . . when I lost her a part of me died."

Malcolm remained quiet knowing there was more to come.

Luther released a heavy breath, reaching beside him to pick up the 5"x7" photograph of his wife holding Malcolm as a newborn. "I promised you I would never marry again," he spoke softly but gruffly to the woman smiling up at him from the photo.

Seeing his father, this man he always thought of as great and strong, near tears shook Malcolm and he took a moment to compose himself with steadying breaths. "Dad, it's over twenty years since Mama died. I know she would never want you to remain alone. You deserve a good woman to love you and be *here* to love you just as much as you love her. You deserve a romance with more than just memories, Pops."

"Elaine's a good woman, you know. She's good to me," Luther admitted, wiping his eyes with the back of his large hands.

"I know that, Pop." Malcolm stood, walking over to clasp his father's shoulder with a strong grasp.

Luther sat the picture back on the end table. "I just never thought I'd meet a woman good enough to break that promise, son."

"Until now?" Malcolm asked with hope, wanting his father to be happy.

Luther released a breath that was heavy with his thoughts, his decisions. He nodded, feeling more confident in his choice. "Until now," he stated with a firmness, turning to look over the chair at his son.

"Then let's go man, you probably got Elaine 'bout to act a fool," Malcolm teased to lighten the moment.

"She reminds me a lot of your mother," Luther said, rising from his chair. "And if that daughter of hers stays out of town, we'll be just fine."

"Tell me about it," Malcolm agreed, with a laugh.

"What did I do to get such a great son?" Luther asked, pulling his son into a bear hug that Malcolm gladly returned.

"You set the example, Pop, and I love you for it."

Serena stood in her bedroom window and watched the activity as the last-minute preparations were made to transform the backyard into the ideal scene for a fall wedding. Luckily, the weather was nice for a Northeast day in late November. Still, they rented a nice-sized tent equipped with a heating unit to knock off some of the chill. The tent was already set up for the wedding and the casual buffet-style reception to follow.

Serena held the dress she'd chosen to wear across her arm and let her body lean against the window with a soft smile. She felt like she was in a different time and place. Over a decade ago it had been her day to wed a man she loved to distraction.

Things had been so different back then. Young, filled with hope and dreams of forever. Happily ever after.

In truth they should have listened to all of the naysayers. They had all been right: too young, too broke, too immature, not ready for marriage.

Maybe, just maybe, if they had been more patient and not given in to their desire to be "grown," things would've turned out differently for them.

The strong, mature, level-headed man Malcolm was today was nothing like the rash and irrational boy she married. And true, she was far gone from the young girl wanting to have it all: the husband, the wild partying girlfriends, and freedom from Auntie's old-school rules.

Still, nothing could change what Malcolm did. There was no excuse for that.

Maybe—

"No," Serena whispered aloud, clinging to her anger as she moved from the window and the wedding scene unfolding below.

No time for maybe, what-if, could have, nor would have.

She didn't want Malcolm back in her life and was positive he felt the same about her.

Still, he was fine and she was quite familiar with his prowess in bed. That man had made it his business to learn how to please and ten years *had* to have aged him like a fine wine—just better with time.

Serena shivered and pressed her thighs together

tightly to stop her moist mound from throbbing as she remembered the feel of Malcolm's lips and tongue pressed intimately against and then *inside* her core.

The night of the winter storm nothing at all had mattered but those heated moments between them. Not the past, not the future. Just the now.

Time for some truth. Even after she pleaded with him to leave her be, Serena had hoped he would come back to her, kiss her, touch her, make love to her.

Okay, maybe she wasn't the smartest tack in the box for letting her ex-husband get a taste of her goodies after what he did to her.

It was hard to deny the man's appeal, especially with him walking out of the shower with a towel wrapped around his hips just one pull away from being nude. Or walking into the den to find him doing sit-ups shirtless. Or walking into the kitchen in the morning to find him in nothing but his boxers as he scrambled eggs. Or just the memories of the steamy moments they shared coming back to her at odd moments of the day.

Auaah!

Mama James, you sweet little devil you.

Fine, she'd admit it.

She wanted Malcolm.

She dreamed of having Malcolm.

She wanted to bathe that sexy body and then dry him with nothing but her lips before she then ravaged him until he couldn't walk for a week.

Damn.

She refused to give in to her desires and her dreams—no matter how badly she wanted to strip him naked, tie him spread-eagle to the bed while she rode him like a bronco.

Serena flushed with embarrassment at her thoughts.

* * *

Malcolm finished instructing one of his assistants on which shots of the wedding he wanted video-taped. He was heading back into the house to double check on the groom when he spotted Miracle moving through the wedding guests. He swore she was headed in his direction and he steeled himself for the pressure she was putting on him.

When she walked past him and muttered, "Fake ass Spike Lee," Malcolm was pleased—and a little confused—by her change in behavior. It seems the chase was off and frankly, he didn't have the time, energy, or inclination to figure out why.

He had just walked through the side door into the kitchen to jog up the stairs when the faint scent of a sweet and subtle perfume surrounded him. The softness of cashmere fluttered against his hand.

Malcolm looked up, surprised to find Serena standing on the step just above him. They almost collided. "Hey Serena," he said, dropping down a step to take her all in.

Damn, he thought. *Serena looks good.*

Her auburn hair fell in soft curls around her face. Her makeup was elaborate and beautiful, with expressive and dramatic eye shadow and soft lips tinted with peach gloss.

But it was the dress. No, correction, it was Serena *in* the dress that caused Malcolm's heart to swell before it pounded in his chest like it wanted to break free.

The strapless cashmere dress of pale yellow was the perfect complement to her bronzed caramel complexion. The material skimmed her curves perfectly, and the matching shrug she wore to protect her arms only served to highlight her round shoulders and delicate collarbone further. The dress stopped just above her knees, leaving her long, shapely legs and calves to be ogled by his appreciating eye.

"Damn, Serena," he said aloud, voicing his thoughts in a deep voice filled with his awareness and appreciation of just how fine she looked.

"You don't look half bad yourself, Saint James," she said huskily and honestly, her eyes warming to the sight of his sexy, bald-headed self in a tailored tuxedo.

Their eyes locked.

A desire to grab her close and kiss her deeply filled him with a quickness and his eyes warmed with the heat of his desire. "Serena—"

"When you and Blondie play footsies you really need to explain the difference between documentaries and music videos," Serena told him, sidestepping him to descend the stairs.

"Blondie? Music videos? Footsies? What the hell—" Malcolm slid his hands into his pockets as he turned on the stair to follow Serena with his eyes. His eyes dipped to watch the material caress her full bottom and his member jumped to life.

Malcolm looked down at his crotch. "We're in trouble."

"Weddings are a joyous occasion. A chance to celebrate the loving union between a man and a woman. A marriage is a more serious matter and one not to be entered into lightly. It is a commitment made not just before family and friends, but God. Respect thy union and it shall last a lifetime. Ephesians, chapter four verses two and three reads: 'Be completely humble and gentle; be patient, bearing with one another in love. Make every effort to keep the unity of the spirit through peace.' Remember what it is you fell in love with, work on your marriage, and do not give up on it so easily when the path gets rocky and you'll be rewarded and blessed with a lifelong companion . . ."

As the minister looked deeply into Luther and Elaine's eyes as he spoke, Serena's eyes drifted to Malcolm from where she sat at the second round table in the front. She was startled to find that he turned suddenly and locked those intense, deep-set ebony eyes on her.

For the life of her she couldn't look away.

Remember what it is you fell in love with, work on your marriage, and do not give up on it so easily when the path gets rocky and you'll be rewarded and blessed with a lifelong companion . . .

Malcolm stood by as his father and Elaine turned to each and began to exchange their wedding vows in emotional tones, but it was the minister's heartfelt words of advice on the commitment to marriage that echoed in his head.

Do not give up on it so easily . . .

Instinctively he looked over his shoulder as his eyes sought Serena in the crowd and found her with ease. When she turned to look at him as well, Malcolm was filled with regret.

They both took their marriage lightly.

They forgot all of the million and one things they loved about one another.

They pushed aside their dreams of owning their own home and having babies together.

They gave up far too easily . . .

Serena sipped deeply from her flute of champagne as she watched the intimate crowd of well-wishers doing the electric slide on the dance floor at the back end of the tent. She was trying her best to forget the preacher's words. They haunted her with their ring of truth.

They hadn't fought for their love, their friendship, their dreams . . . their marriage.

She was feeling a lot of emotions that had her confused. Memories of her own wedding, regrets on the destruction of a great childhood friendship, her constant awareness and desire for Malcolm . . .

"Hey, whassup."

Serena looked up from staring into the center of the amber liquid of her flute to find *him* standing before her.

Her heart drummed an up-tempo beat.

Malcolm smiled down at her, looking a thousand times better than a GQ model. "I've come for my dance. Atlanta won, remember?"

Serena felt breathless and weak, but she hid it so well as she rose, tucked her purse under her arm and strutted ahead of him onto the crowded dance floor.

Malcolm dropped his head and smiled as he followed at a leisurely pace, enjoying the view of her hips swaying left to right.

Serena chose a spot and turned to face him as he came to her with a confident swagger that drew long stares from women in the crowd. "You have a little audience," she told him, motioning her head to the table of three women staring and whispering in their direction.

Malcolm didn't spare them a glance. "There isn't a woman here to rival you."

"Flirt."

Malcolm just laughed.

"You know this is the only way you'll be in my arms, right?"

"Don't be so sure, Serena."

Just as Malcolm placed his all-too-familiar hands on the small of her back and pulled her body close to his, the jazz band began to play "Always and Forever" by Heatwave.

Serena leaned back in Malcolm's arm to look up into his eyes. It was *their* song. A song directly tied to some of the greatest moments from the Malcolm & Serena days.

The night Malcolm proposed at the prom.

Their first dance as Mr. and Mrs. Malcolm Saint James.

A sweet serenade during so many occasions when they made love during their marriage.

"I requested this song," he whispered.

"I figured you did."

"I wanted to remember one of the best nights of my life."

"Shut up, Malcolm, and just dance."

Malcolm winked at her and pulled her closer.

Slowly they rocked, their bodies falling into a natural rhythm together. That awareness between them rising.

"We gave up too easily, Serena," he whispered fiercely into her ear.

Serena closed her eyes against a dart of pain. She let her cheek rest against his chest as she closed her eyes, inhaled deeply of his scent, and let herself be taken to another time and place.

Interlude

I Do

1994

It was her wedding day. In no time at all she would become Mrs. Malcolm Saint James and there was nothing she wanted more than to be his wife.

Still, she was nervous, and what woman in her position wouldn't be?

Monique said she was crazy to give up her freedom.

Malcolm's father kept asking them if they'd lost their minds.

Auntie pleaded with them to wait because they were so young.

Even the minister counseled against it.

What if they were right?

"Ready?"

Serena turned and smiled softly as the wedding planner Mama James hired pulled back the sheer white curtains blocking off her beautiful backyard wedding. As she stepped forward to begin her walk down the aisle alone, her eyes took in everything through her veil.

The white aisle stretched before her littered with soft red rose petals.

The floral decorations in every available nook and corner.

Their family and friends rising from their cloth-covered seats to turn and face her.

Monique stood in her place as the maid of honor and mouthed "You go, girl."

Auntie's eyes were misty as she blew her nose in her lace handkerchief.

Mama James gave her a spunky thumbs up, looking regal and grand in her silver suit and matching hat.

Luther motioned for her to put her head up and Serena did with a smile.

And then Malcolm.

Her Malcolm.

He looked so fine in his tuxedo and Serena felt her heart swell with love for him.

Malcolm smiled in return and then motioned with his hand for her to come to him.

At that moment as her eyes locked with his, her worries and fears evaporated like a fine mist. Her grip on her bouquet was no longer as tight, her heart's furious pounding eased, and the butterflies in her stomach fluttered away.

I love him. I really love him. And everything is going to be all right. Her heart swelled with emotions and she paced herself to keep from running to him.

Malcolm's first sight of Serena standing at the opposite end of the aisle in her white flowing dress caused a myriad of emotions to fill his chest. Desire, happiness, pleasure, a little fear, but mostly love.

Today was years in the making and it couldn't have come any sooner for him. Today was the start of the rest of his and Serena's life together. He would sleep with Serena. Wake up to Serena. Live every day with Serena. Make love to Serena.

He smiled widely and brightly at that last one.

True, they were starting off just a little rough having to live with his grandmother, but they would both work hard to build a better life for themselves.

Serena reached him and he offered her his hand. She took it and he squeezed it tightly.

"Hey beautiful," he said lightly to her.

"Hey you, Saint James," she whispered with a smile back, sounding out of breath.

Clutching each other's slender hands, they faced the minister at the altar, both taking a deep steadying breath as they prepared to make their vows to love, honor, and cherish until death.

Chapter 10

Although he slept in the nude, had only a cotton sheet spread across his bed, and had a circulating fan lightly blowing cool air across the room, Malcolm was heated. It had nothing at all to do with the now fully functioning boiler helping to pump heat throughout the house.

Malcolm tossed and turned inside that world where people lay half awake and half asleep.

Punching his pillows for comfort he flopped onto his stomach. Moments later he flopped onto his back, placing his hands behind his smooth bald head. He opened his eyes and saw the moon's beam illuminate the tenting of the sheet from his throbbing erection.

Here he was, a grown behind man, lying in bed with a hard-on like a horny teenager.

Serena made him feel that way.

The sight of her fresh out of the shower with nothing but a towel to shield her nakedness from him.

The scent of her perfume around the house.

The way her pajama bottoms hung low emphasizing her hips and the deep curve of her buttocks.

Her nipples pressed against a T-shirt as she lounged about the house without a bra.

And how she felt in his arms as they danced at the reception last week.

But there were other things heavy on his mind than just how sexy his ex was. Things he had long since given up on.

Or so he thought.

Malcolm kicked the sheets from his sculpted body. He left the bed, glad that his erection had eased. Not bothering to turn on the lights, he moved under the cloak of darkness to retrieve his laptop.

As a wedding present to his father and new step-mother, who were returning from their honeymoon tomorrow, he was personally putting together a montage of their wedding day.

Malcolm smiled at the sight of his father delivering a sound slap to Elaine's bottom with a wide roguish grin. Elaine swatted at him playfully and halfheartedly before blessing him with a soft smile and an even softer kiss.

His hawklike eyes focused on a shapely figure strutting across the dance floor in the distance. His heart double pumped in recognition of Serena in that hellacious dress. He leaned forward to watch as his image strolled across the dance floor with ease to pull Serena into his arms with a smile.

Working the mouse on the keyboard, Malcolm paused the video and zoomed in on them. At that moment, captured eternally on video, Serena was leaning back slightly in his arms and looking up into his face with a beguiling smile that tugged at his heart.

Remember what it is you fell in love with, work on your marriage, and do not give up on it so easily when the path gets rocky and you'll be rewarded and blessed with a lifelong companion . . .

Malcolm's eyes squinted as he sat back against the padded headboard and locked those intense hawklike eyes on Serena's tempting face.

Serena's thoughts were heavy as well, as sleep eluded her. Heavy as all get out with Malcolm Saint James and that was more frustrating than words could ever express.

Everyday living with him, being so acutely aware of him, and wanting him was weakening her resolve and blurring the line she'd sworn she'd never cross with her ex-husband ever again. Ever.

Needing some help to keep her from stripping free of her clothes and climbing into Malcolm's bed just as naked as she pleased, Serena reached for her cell phone on the nightstand.

Nothing like a quick convo with Monique to freshen her disdain of Malcolm.

Serena turned on the lamp with one hand and dialed her friend's home number with the other. As it rang, her eyes sought and found the clock.

It was 10:43 P.M.

Serena patted the silk scarf tied around her head as she listened to the incessant ringing. "Where are you Monique?" she asked aloud, looking down at her fingernails which were in bad need of a manicure.

Monique's answering machine clicked on.

"Hey, this is Monique. I've made some changes in my life and . . . if I don't call you back, you're one of them."

Beep.

Serena rolled her eyes heavenward. "Monique, what man are you tricking up on a big Sunday night? Call me, girl."

She closed her cell phone.

Serena grabbed her toiletry kit and headed to the bathroom for a relaxing bath to ease the foolish thoughts she was having about Malcolm. After twisting her newly weaved hair into a loose top knot, Serena undressed and slipped beneath the steamy depths of the bath water scented with citrus oils.

Letting her head fall back against the tiled wall, she inhaled deeply of her favorite scent, wanting to be released of the maddening desire to rush into Malcolm's bedroom, arouse him to hardness, and ride him until they both were spent.

"You horny little girl," she chided herself, sinking a bit lower beneath the water.

She tried to focus her thoughts elsewhere: her continuing plans for her salon—regardless of where she decided to open it; scouting the cosmetology schools for at least one new hairstylist with promise who was eager to sign on with a new salon; another salon her realtor wanted to show her next week.

Still, she thought of him. Not just his physical appeal but things she noticed about him while they shared the house the past month, some familiar to her and some not.

His dedication to his work was inspiring.

His love of his family was touching.

His deep appreciation of music and the hip-hop culture she also loved.

His confidence. His charisma. His serious nature. His passion.

Finding the gentle lapping of the water against her sensitive nipples and core only intensified her arousal, Serena picked up her scented soap and washcloth to finish her bath. The slick feel of the sudsy rag against her core wasn't much help in easing her lust either.

As she rose from the water she reached for her

plush towel, barely drying the moisture from her body before she stepped out of the tub and into her satin robe. Tying it loosely, she quickly straightened the bathroom.

Just as she stepped into the hall Malcolm stepped out of his bedroom just as naked as the day he was born.

Serena's eyes perused him quickly just before Malcolm covered his privates—as best he could—with his hands. That telling bud between her legs was swollen with a heated rush of awareness and need. She couldn't take her eyes off the sculpted and well-defined lines of his body.

"Didn't know you were still up," Malcolm explained, his dark eyes dropping to take in the intimate way the satin clung to the deep curves of her body, particularly each full swell of her breasts.

He knew she was naked beneath it and his member hardened on its own accord.

Serena saw the heat in Malcolm's eyes as electricity crackled between them. Desire was ready to explode. A thirst craved to be quenched.

Her eyes dropped down and she watched in open fascination as his member lengthened with hardness before her very eyes. His hand could no longer cover nor contain the thick ten inches and Serena knew right then, right now . . . she *had* to have him.

Malcolm stepped forward and pulled Serena into his arms with a low growl of hunger for her.

Serena welcomed his heated embrace, pressing every delicious curve of her body against his lean hardness as she shivered with want. It had been too long. *Far* too long.

Their lips locked hungrily. Their movements were as frantic as their heartbeats with the pent-up desire they created in each other during the past month together in the house. Shaking hands stroked and caressed every part of the other's body.

Serena's robe flew open in the fray and they both moaned deeply at the feel of her warm breasts against his muscled chest. His hard member throbbed against the soft cushion of her belly.

A perfect fit.

Malcolm ran his hands across Serena's bottom, firmly grasping each cheek as he hoisted her up his body with ease.

Serena suckled his tongue deeply with a purr as she locked her legs behind his waist and hugged his strong neck with her arms.

Malcolm backed into his bedroom, nearly sending them both tumbling over a chair. He righted himself and shifted to the left to continue backward as he frantically reached out with one hand for his wallet sitting on the nightstand.

Serena broke their kiss and used her hands to guide Malcolm's full lips to one of her aching breasts. As he took one taut nipple into his eager mouth, Serena arched her back and flung her head back with her mouth gaped as the soft tendrils of her auburn tresses tickled the small of her back.

Even as he circled that mocha nipple with his tongue the way he knew she loved, Malcolm removed a condom from his wallet and worked open the foil to sheath himself for their protection.

He stepped back until his back was braced against the closet door and Serena unwrapped her legs and braced her knees against the door on either side of his body. Serena was on fire as she let the robe slide down her arms to the floor and placed her hands against the wall on either side of his head. "Now, Malcolm," she demanded huskily as a fine sheen of perspiration coated her bronzed skin.

Malcolm lifted Serena up slightly by her hips with strong hands, fitting the tip of his shaft to the opening of her core.

Their eyes locked and held.

"Ready?" he asked.

"Been ready," she answered.

He brought Serena down upon him with one fierce movement to surround him with her tight warmth until he filled her with his entire shaft.

They both gasped hotly.

Malcolm felt near spilling his seed so very soon and fought for control. He looked up at her, as she began to ride him, her breasts moving in countermotion to her body as she pushed him over the edge. What little control he had of his member flew out the window.

She bit her bottom lip in pure pleasure as she rode hard, enjoying the feel of him against her slick walls and stroking her swollen pink bud, seeking and finding the first warm waves of release as it began to course over her body.

"Yes, Malcolm, yes. Hmm . . . hmmm . . . hmmmmm . . . hmmmmmmmmmmmmmmmmm . . ."

"Se-se-re-re-re-re-re-re-re—," he stuttered as his member jolted with each spasm releasing his seed. He clamped his mouth down on her breasts to keep from sounding like a stuttering fool as he let his head fall back against the wall.

They clutched each other tightly, both working their hips at a frenzied pace to their passion, their bodies drenched in sweat, their hearts beating loudly in unison until they were sated and spent.

Malcolm placed tender kisses along Serena's collarbone and neck as he carried her to the bed and laid her down on it still quivering from her explosive release. Malcolm strode to the bathroom to dispose of their protection and relieve himself. He paused in the mirror to look at his reflection and smiled broadly at what he just shared with Serena.

Where did they go from here? Bed buddies until this little two-month adventure was over? A relationship?

Whoa.

Good sex—no, great sex—was not a basis for a new relationship. Besides he didn't want a relationship, did he? Did she?

There was still so much between them that was unresolved.

The only thing he knew for sure was that he wanted to lie on his bed beside that incredible woman, hold her body close and sleep until his body was reenergized.

Malcolm walked back into his bedroom to find Serena lightly snoring as she lay on her side in the middle of his bed. He pulled on a pair of boxers from his dresser and turned off the lights before climbing in bed behind Serena to spoon her. Soon he joined her in an exhausted sleep and his snores echoed her own.

Luther lit his cigar as soon as he stepped out onto the balcony of his honeymoon suite. Even at midnight, Jamaica was beautiful. He leaned against the balcony in nothing but his robe and enjoyed the scenic view of the ocean and the taste of his new favorite treat: Harvill-flavored Jamaican cigars. Tonight he inhaled deeply of the hand-rolled treasure seasoned with Passion Rum. He hated to exhale.

Although Malcolm didn't smoke, Luther had purchased a box for his son. Maybe there would be something to celebrate when they returned. Something like Malcolm and Serena's reconciling.

Who knew?

Wouldn't shock him one bit if—or rather—*when* they did get back together. Those two might've finally decided to stop playing mad, and also stop playing games, and work like two grown people to get back together. Either way, he wasn't sticking his nose in too much. It was up to them.

Sure, he thought his mother's plan might just work, but would he have masterminded this elaborate scheme to play matchmaker?

Definitely not.

Still, he thought it was working.

As irritating as Miracle was, she was a fine looking young woman and Luther sat back and watched as his son didn't make move number one to get some of her rhythm.

And anyone could see that his son and ex-daughter-in-law were itching like a case of the crabs to get in bed and sweat out all that phony hostility. Their noses were wide open.

Beside the physical attraction, Luther had spent enough time at the house to see that Serena had matured over the years—just like Malcolm.

If only they had waited like Vanessa and I'd said.

Luther thought of Serena's aunt/guardian Vanessa Freeman. Vanessa had been one hella fine, big-boned, high-yellow woman. Being a man who always appreciated a beautiful sistah, Luther had made a play for her, offering a night of dinner, dancing, and more.

Vanessa looked at him with a cocked brow and said in that sweet, husky voice of hers: "Luther Saint James, don't start none, won't be none. Just carry you and your drama out my house this instant. I'll be damned if I'm one of your stable, you wannabe pimp. Now get!"

And "get" he had, as she raised her cast iron skillet up to shake at him.

Luther laughed at the memory. *Ole Vanessa.*

"Luther?"

He turned to find Elaine rolling over in bed. She sat up and he could see the outline of her full breasts through her gown. Nice sight indeed. He reached into the pocket of his robe for one of his Viagra pills—or Blue Heaven as he liked to call it.

"Luther, were you laughing out there by your lonesome?" she called over to him.

"Yeah," he called back, stalling because it always took exactly thirteen minutes for his little blue friend to kick in. "Just thinking 'bout old times, that's all."

"Oh," she said, stretching her arms above her head, which brought his attention back to those breasts he loved.

Deciding some foreplay with his beautiful wife until he got revved up wasn't a bad thing, Luther put out his cigar.

"You coming, baby?"

"Not yet, but we both will be in about nine minutes."

Elaine laughed softly as Luther walked back into the bedroom and dropped his robe. He climbed onto the bed between her lavender-scented thighs with a tigerlike growl.

Hamp poured himself a shot of Crown Royal in the study of his split-level condo. He carried his drink to his desk, taking a deep sip before setting it on a coaster and himself in the leather chair.

Lying on the center of his mahogany desk were two unopened letters with Olivia's bold, slanted handwriting on the envelopes. One for Serena. The other for Malcolm.

He released a heavy breath as his eyes shifted to the

5"x7" photo of Olivia that he kept on his desk. He missed his friend dearly.

But then again, Olivia had been so much more to him than just a companion. During every bit of their thirty-year friendship, Hamp had loved Olivia to distraction.

He never revealed that he was in love with her to another living soul, not even Olivia. He kept his ardor a secret and now that she was gone, he regretted that very deeply.

With sadness weighing his thin shoulders down, Hamp reached for the photo and studied her with a smile. "You were a remarkable woman, Livvie, and I loved you. No, I love you still."

Hamp reached for his drink and swallowed down the tears he felt rising.

Losing his taste for the drink, he set it aside, his eyes falling to the envelopes again. "Remarkable and so wise."

He specifically remembered the day Olivia handed him those envelopes. He had visited her at home that day and they were sitting in the den, her favorite room in the house.

"I'm feeling like that cook I like on cable. You know, Emeril? Sometimes you got to kick it up a notch."

She passed him the two envelopes.

"Once they're in that house and you see any sign that those two are cracking, I want you to give 'em their letters. And they're not to discuss what's in those letters with anyone."

Hamp chuckled lightly at the memory. Olivia got what she wanted, *when* she wanted it.

Well, after witnessing Malcolm and Serena giving each other goo-goo eyes during the wedding ceremony and then seeing them get lost in each other as they danced at the reception, Hamp definitely felt it was time to kick it up a notch.

* * *

Serena awakened hours later entangled in Malcolm's strong arms and legs. Smacking her lips at the bad taste of sleep in her mouth, she gingerly freed herself from his limbs and rose from the bed. In the darkness she bent down to search for her robe.

Her hand had just clutched it when the room was suddenly bathed in light. Serena looked up into Malcolm's face as he lay on his side looking up at her with that familiar heat in his ebony eyes.

"Come back to bed, Serena."

She rose and slipped on her robe, tying the belt securely around her waist. "No, Malcolm," she answered softly, turning to leave the room.

Malcolm flung back the sheet and sprang from the bed to clasp his hand around Serena's wrist, stopping her exit. "Don't do this—"

Serena turned to face him with an incredulous face. "Don't do what, Malcolm? Huh?"

Malcolm's eyes cooled. "Don't make me feel like I forced you."

"No, you didn't force me. I was just as into it as you were, wanting it just as much," she admitted, all too aware of his fingertips pressed against her skin.

"Damn right."

"But it won't happen again," she finished as she met his eyes. "It was a mistake."

"A damn good mistake," Malcolm said with a roguish grin that made him even more handsome. "One I wouldn't mind making again."

As Malcolm, in all his sexy nakedness, stepped closer to her, Serena sidestepped him even as a jolt of awareness shot through her.

She worked free of his grasp on her wrist. "You

didn't deserve the taste of all this goodness, please don't expect seconds."

Malcolm rubbed his hand over his smooth bald head as he looked down at her. "Deserve?"

Serena crossed her arms over her chest, trying so hard not to let her eyes drift over his nearly naked frame. "Damn right."

Malcolm looked at his ex-wife like she was crazy. "You know what, Serena. I'm tired of you making me feel like I ruined our marriage all by my damn self."

Serena's mouth dropped open as she eyed him in astonishment.

"When are you going to fess up to your part in all of it?" Malcolm asked.

Serena's emotions swung erratically in a matter of seconds, but she snatched at the one she was most familiar with when it came to Malcolm Saint James: anger. "How dare you, Malcolm. After what you did to me you have the audacity, the bigheaded nerve, the foolishness to . . . to . . ."

Her words drifted off as tears welled up in her throat. She closed her eyes and breathed deeply to regain her composure because she was not going to let a single tear fall. She turned her back to him as she found herself failing at doing just that.

Damn. Malcolm released a heavy breath and stepped forward to grasp Serena's shoulders.

She swung around and pushed him away from her with both hands. "Stay away from me, Saint James," she told him over her shoulder as she opened the bedroom door wide.

Malcolm waved his hand dismissively as he walked back to his bed. "Go ahead, Serena. Keep running from the truth," he called over his shoulder.

Serena froze in the doorway.

"Same bs from when we were married. I was sick of it then and I'm sick of it right now."

Serena whirled around dramatically, her robe flaring a bit behind her. "I don't give a damn what you're sick of, then or now. I didn't deserve how you did me, Malcolm Saint James."

Malcolm blew air though his teeth as he reached down to pick up his discarded covers from the floor.

"Not only was I your wife, I was your friend."

He paused in arranging the covers on his bed to glance over at her.

"Why, Malcolm?" she asked. "How in the hell could you, of all people, do me," she poked her chest with her forefinger, "like that?"

Interlude

I Don't

1995

Brrnnnggg.

Serena wished she had a gun to stop the incessant ringing of the telephone. She'd been over to Monique's house braiding her mother's hair until about one A.M. and then she'd argued with Malcolm until two A.M. about how bad it looked for a married woman to just be getting home that time of night. The last thing she wanted to do was be awakened before her body said it was okay.

Brrnnnggg.

One more ring and Serena was glad for the invention of the answering machine.

"You got Serena and Malcolm, we're not able to take your call. Leave a message."

Beep.

"Hey, Serena. It's me—"

Serena turned over at the sound of Malcolm's voice. He had slept on the chair after their argument and left for work without saying "boo" to her. She reached out for the phone.

"Just calling to see how your interview for the job went—"

Her hand jerked back like the phone was fire. *Damn. I forgot about that.*

"We gotta talk when I get home. I love you, Serena, but things got to change. Um. I, ah, I'm on my break. I'll see you later."

Serena dragged her body to a sitting position. She looked at the clock on the nightstand. It was noon and her interview at Pathmark on Lyons Avenue for a cashier position had been at nine.

If she admitted to Malcolm that she messed up yet another job interview then she knew it was a bonafide argument when he got home. Just one more to add to the ever-increasing list of disputes and disagreements.

When they first got married, everything had been the bomb diggity. They lived with Mama James until they could get their own apartment and once they were in their own place all hell seemed to break loose.

A lot of the things Mama James used to take care of, Malcolm expected her to take over. She wasn't aware that she signed on for a life of cooking, cleaning, and saluting the self-proclaimed king of the castle.

It was true what they said, you never really know a person until you lived with him. And now she knew Malcolm was bossy, demanding, chauvinistic and full of criticism.

"You can't cook."

"You can't clean."

"Your friends are no good."

"You *need* a job."

Brrnnnggg.

Serena's eyes darted to the phone. She watched it warily, glad when the ringing stopped.

"*You got Serena and Malcolm, we're not able to take your call. Leave a message.*"

"Serena? Where you at girl? This—"

Serena snatched up the phone. "Hey, Monique," she said, settling back down on the bed.

"Screening calls?"

"Sum'n like that. What's up?"

"Nothing, just chillin'. We're thinking 'bout going to a party at Rutgers tonight. You down?"

"Nah. Girl, please, Malcolm still mad over me getting home so late from your house last night," Serena admitted.

"You're married or in jail? Ain't no way a man gone tell me what to do. First you went from your aunt having you on lockdown to Malcolm holding the dang key."

Living with Auntie had deprived Serena of all the hanging out a lot of kids in their neighborhood got to enjoy. She was always in the house before dark. If she went to parties, it had to be with Malcolm and even then they had to be home by eleven. If you lived in Auntie's house, then you played by her rules.

Serena missed her something awful. She passed away three months after Serena and Malcolm's wedding. Serena was now just able to think about her without breaking down in tears.

Serena felt annoyed by Monique's blasé reference to her beloved aunt, but she ignored it.

"Anyway, I'm gone clean up this house and look in the papers for a job."

"A job!"

Many times in the past Monique proclaimed that if Malcolm wanted to live like the Cleavers on *Leave It to Beaver*, then he needed to step up like Ward and be the sole provider.

"I better go, girl," Serena said, shifting her body to the edge of the bed.

"We're going to play Bingo later, call me if you wanna go and I'll swing by and get you. Oh, and tell Malcolm I said to go to hell."

"Bye, girl," Serena said, rising from the bed.

Malcolm and Monique absolutely hated each other, always had. He said she was a bad influence and she said he was a control freak. Serena was always refereeing.

She stepped over the pile of clothes she'd separated yesterday to wash. And she meant to do just that . . . until Monique picked her to go to the mall.

That reminded her of the new high-top Reeboks she bought. True, she dipped into the bill money Malcolm gave her but she would juggle some things, do a couple of heads, and make it all work out somehow.

Feeling guilty about missing the job interview, Serena decided to clean up their small one-bedroom apartment and even took out chicken to fry for dinner.

Okay, truth be told she did need a job to help Malcolm with the bills, right now they were struggling and living check to check to make it. They were arguing. Mad at each other. They weren't happy. There was more bad than good.

Serena picked up the wedding photo from the nightstand and smiled a little at the memory. They had their ups and downs but she loved her handsome husband. They had big plans for the future. And she was willing to fight for that future because above all she loved him.

Malcolm used his key to enter the apartment. He was surprised to find the living room no longer looking like a train went through it. As he walked through the rest of the house he saw that his wife's cleaning spurt didn't reach any further.

No dinner was fixed, although chicken still thawed in the sink. Piles of dirty clothes were still on the bedroom floor. The bed looked like they'd just climbed out of it.

And Serena wasn't home. He found a note in the bedroom saying she went to do someone's hair. He was tired of the haphazard beautician crap. It was not steady income and then what little money she did make she spent as fast as she got it.

And if she saw them struggling until he could get a better job why wouldn't she work like they talked about before they got married?

Sometimes he felt like Serena was using him. He worked his butt off at Mickey Dees, paying the bills as best he could while looking for a better job, going without things while Serena spent the day hanging out with her friends.

She was nothing at all like the wife he thought she would be. She wouldn't do what he said to do. Wouldn't work. Wouldn't clean or cook. Had a funky attitude all the time.

Didn't the Bible speak of a wife obeying her husband? Wasn't it his right as a man—a husband—to have his wife do as he asked?

All of a sudden she was into parties and hanging out with her friends or gossiping on the phone with her friends. Things she never did before.

Well, things Auntie wouldn't let her do.

Malcolm was frustrated and fed up with Serena.

Thoughts of them separating crossed his mind more and more. Last night after their argument, as he struggled to find comfort on their sofa, he had made the decision to tell Serena that things were not working out. He just didn't want to be married anymore. And that was the gospel.

He loved her but it was clear that marriage and the everyday grind of living together was not working. Instead of becoming closer they were drifting apart. They both spent more time with their friends than they did with each other.

Needing to vent, Malcolm picked up the phone to call his father. Seconds later he looked down at the phone in his hand.

It was off.

How could that be when he gave Serena bill money just last week?

Malcolm slumped his thin frame down onto the sofa, his thoughts heavy as the minutes slipped into hours. The sky became dark.

He waited until he could wait no more.

He spent the next hour packing as many of his things as he could and still she hadn't returned.

It was evident to him that Serena and he didn't want the same type of marriage—probably never did.

He was damn tired of trying to make it work.

Malcolm swung his duffel bag onto his shoulder, removed the key from his ring, dropped it to the coffee table, and walked out on his marriage without one look back.

Serena waved good-bye to Monique as she pulled off in her mother's sky-blue Escort hatchback. She looked up to the window of their second-floor apartment and saw that their lights were on.

She had been cleaning up the apartment just as she planned when Monique called and asked if Serena could do her aunt's hair. Remembering the money she needed to pay the phone bill, Serena had told Monique to scoop her up.

Serena entered the apartment and for some reason the first thing her eyes took in was the key sitting on the coffee table. "Malcolm?" she called.

Frowning, she walked around the small apartment, checking what few rooms they had. When she entered the bedroom, her mouth fell open. The closet door was open and she could see that the side where his clothes usually hung was empty. Her eyes darted to the piles of dirty clothes and saw they were much smaller now that they were devoid of his items. She went back into the bathroom and opened the medicine cabinet. His cologne and other personal items were gone as well.

By now her heart was racing and alarm filled her. "What the hell?" she muttered.

Malcolm left her?

Serena ran to the phone and picked it up, throwing it away in disgust when she realized that the phone company had turned it off.

Serena raced out of the apartment and down the stairs to the pay phone on the corner. Frantically she dug in her pocket for change, ramming the coins into the tiny slot with shaking fingers. She dialed Mama James' house as fast as she could.

"Hello."

"Mama James? Mama James, this . . . this is Serena. Is Malcolm there?" she asked, trying to calm down.

"Yes baby, he's here. What's going on? Why does he have all his clothes? Are you two fighting again?"

Serena closed her eyes and bit her bottom lip. "Yes Ma'am, but can I talk to him . . . please?"

"Hold on, baby. I'll get him."

Serena felt lost and she tried to compose her words as she waited for her husband to pick up the phone.

"Serena?"

"Yes, ma'am?"

"He won't come to the phone, baby. He's hole up in that room listening to that ole rap music. What in the world is going on?"

"I came home and he was gone," Serena said, her voice almost as numb as she felt.

"Come over here right now and get your husband, Serena," Mama James ordered in that regal, not-to-be-ignored voice of hers.

Serena shook her head, embarrassed by Malcolm's treatment of her. "No, ma'am. You tell Malcolm that he ran away to your house and at your house is where he needs to stay."

"Serena, I'll talk to him—"

"Good-bye, Mama James."

Serena hung up the phone and swallowed back the rest of her tears. People passing by on the street looked at her oddly, but she held her head high and ignored them as she made her way back to her apartment.

As soon as she closed the front door, her show of bravado failed. Her chest began to heave as she gasped for air. She felt lightheaded and dropped to the floor, curling into a ball as her body shook with tears.

Chapter 11

"Not a good-bye. Not a note. Nothing," Serena spat with anger in her eyes.

Malcolm flinched at the emotions raging in her eyes. Yes, he knew she had pain but so did he. "We've argued about this before when we first broke up, Serena. Why keep bringing it up?"

"You *left* me," she told him, her voice accusing.

Malcolm never saw the shoe coming until it flew past his head with a *whoosh*. When he saw Serena bending down to scoop up its match, he barely ducked in time and outstretched his hand. "If you throw that shoe at me I'm going to—"

Whoosh.

"Serena!" Malcolm roared and then dodged quickly to his left.

Whoosh. An Air Jordan sneaker flew by.

Whoosh. His wallet.

Whoosh. His rodeo-style belt buckle.

Malcolm dodged another item he couldn't even identify and took one lunge forward to bend and scoop Serena up and unceremoniously fling her over his shoulder.

"Put . . . me . . . down, Saint James," she yelled, beating him about the back and shoulders with her balled fists.

"If you keep acting like a child, I'm going to spank you like a child, Serena," he warned darkly.

She felt like twenty different hells flew through her and she continued her barrage in earnest.

Malcolm flinched as one solid little fist hit the middle of his back. He raised one hand and held it one inch from her bottom, "If you hit me again, I'm going to hit you back," he warned, holding her legs firmly against his chest to prevent her from kicking him.

Serena took great pleasure in pummeling his back even more.

Whop. Malcolm delivered one firm and sound smack to Serena's rear.

She froze. It had stung but she refused to show it. "Oh, Negro. No the hell you didn't."

Malcolm shifted his body and released Serena onto the bed on her back and dropped down atop her in one fluid motion. "If you promise to act right, I'll let you up," he told her, looking down into her stoic face.

Serena looked up at him, this handsome and virile man and her anger dissipated into sadness. "After Auntie died, you knew you were all the family I had in this world. All those years as friends and you threw it all out like it was nothing. It was our marriage. Our friendship," she finished with emotion. "Until death do us part, Malcolm. Remember?"

Unable to take the myriad of emotions playing in her eyes like a movie, Malcolm rolled off of her and then sat up on the edge of the bed.

"I felt like you left the marriage way before I left that day, Serena," he insisted in a husky voice as he looked over his shoulder at her. "We weren't happy and that was *both* our faults."

Serena rose from the bed and crossed her arms over her chest. "You were too damn bossy," she countered.

"And you wanted to hang out with your friends," he shot back, putting his elbows on his knees as he locked his fingers in the air between his legs.

Serena looked incredulous. "I . . . was . . . eighteen!" she stressed.

"You were my wife," Malcolm stated simply.

Serena shook her head. "Can you imagine how I felt to come home and your clothes were gone? You snuck away—"

"And you filed for the divorce."

Serena laughed bitterly as she looked down at him. "You damn right I did."

Malcolm felt his ire rise. "You always had a smart mouth."

"So?" she snapped with attitude.

"So it ran me off, that's so."

That hurt, but she hid that as well. "You ran off because you were a little boy playing house. When things didn't go your way you went running to grandma with your trail tucked between your skinny little legs like it was a game."

"No, games are fun and at the end there wasn't a damn thing fun about our marriage," he retorted.

"Okay, fine, Malcolm. I was the worst wife ever, I got your damn point," she said bitterly, as she paced the room.

Malcolm rose from the bed to walk to her.

She snatched away from the grasp of his hands on her shoulders. "It wasn't just you. It was both of us. Everybody was right. We were too young to get married. Point blank."

Serena shook her head. "No."

"What?"

"Regardless of why you ran out on me."

"I kept paying the bills for you, and that was *before* the alimony."

"Big . . . damn . . . deal."

"Serena we've been pissed at each other for years. I left and you got the divorce. In the end neither one of us wanted to be married anymore, Serena."

She looked at him like he had two heads.

"Especially with Monique in your ear dogging me out" he muttered.

True. Serena shifted her eyes from his. "It was your decision to skip out and my decision to file the papers."

"They were three people in our marriage and that's one more than needed," he said pensively, as he started picking up the scattered items Serena had thrown at him.

"If I listened to Monique so much I wouldn't have married you. She warned me not to."

"'Cause she wanted me her damn self   ."

Serena frowned as the rest of his words trailed off. "What are you talking about now? What do you mean she wanted you?"

Malcolm knew Serena well and the fury brewing in her mocha eyes wasn't a good sign—neither was the clenching and unclenching of her fists at her side. The woman could purr like a kitten in pleasure, but was as lethally dangerous as a cougar when angry.

Like right now.

"Monique came at you like that?"

Malcolm knew that the last thing he should be focused on was how devastatingly sexy Serena was as she stood there, her robe nearly bursting open from her heaving chest. Eyes fiery. Lips pursed. Her head cocked to the side. Eyebrow arched.

Sexy as all get out.

"I didn't give her a chance to come at me, but a man knows when he can make a play on a woman and score."

Serena's chest was hot with anger. "Oh really?"

"Trying to make eye contact, licking lips, brushing up against me, bending over in front of me. Some of my boys saw her come-ons too, man, and teased me about it."

"Really?" Serena's voice was dangerously low. "Why didn't you ever tell me? We're you planning on taking her up on it? Did you . . . ever take her up on it?"

"Serena, you were was so caught up in Monique as soon as she moved in the hood. I figured you just wanted a female best friend, to talk to about things we couldn't get down about especially since we were past being buddies by then."

Serena did one of her sistah girl head and eye rolls. "And where in that soliloquy did you answer my question?"

"Talk to me in a better tone, Serena," Malcolm ordered.

"First off," Serena began, holding up one slender finger as she advanced on him. "Negro, *please*. Second off, you just told me my best friend was trying to come at you behind my back *and* you never told me about it until now. Oh, excuse me if I'm not docile."

"This was when she first moved in the neighborhood. And you wouldn't have believed me anyway so I just stayed the hell out of her way."

Serena became swamped with exasperation. "Malcolm, how can you keep telling me about how *I* feel, what *I* want, and how *I* would act? Are you psychic?" she asked as she turned to leave the room. "If so don't quit your day job."

"Just like old times," he muttered darkly as he tossed his shoes into the closet.

Malcolm was going over their conversation when he heard the metal rattle of car keys. His brows furrowed as he leaned over to look out the door at the hall. He saw a shadow of Serena headed down the stairs.

Where's she going this time of the night?

He rushed into a sweat suit and sneakers to take off down the stairs and out the door just as Serena climbed into her car parked in the driveway. Not worrying about the cold air biting him through his clothes, Malcolm dashed across the small lawn to climb into the passenger side.

Serena's head whipped to face him.

Malcolm almost recoiled at the anger he saw. "Where are you going?" he asked, knowing that in the past she could become irrational when angry.

"Over to Monique's," she said calmly. *Too* calmly.

"Serena, it's two in the morning."

"And?"

"Well I'm going with you."

"That's probably best."

Malcolm put on his seatbelt as Serena cranked the car and backed down the drive. He was glad she'd at least taken time to change out of the robe into warm clothing.

"You know this is crazy, right?" he asked, eyeing her stoic face as she drove with speed but not a sign of recklessness.

Serena nodded.

Malcolm's eyes roamed over Serena, pausing at the intimate way her jeans pressed against her thighs like second skin. Thighs that had clutched his sides as she rode him against the wall. His member stirred to life and his hands itched to caress those thighs. He wanted Serena again. She was in his blood.

He thought they would be buried beneath the covers in his bed, creating their own heat. Instead they were in a car heading to confront a woman he'd rather not see ever again if he had a choice.

"I won't be able sleep until I do this," she said suddenly into the quiet intimacy of the car.

Serena knew this excursion was a little reminiscent of her younger days, but the thought that Monique had been in her ear and in her face for all these years bad-talking Malcolm, stirring up drama in their relationship and later their marriage, when she would have scooped Malcolm up for herself with half the chance was bothering her.

Serena believed Malcolm. The man was many things but a liar wasn't one of them. To be honest she had seen Monique do a couple of things that a less trusting fool like herself would have called her on. And that's why she was in her car, with the scent of her sexscapade with Malcolm still clinging to her as she headed to confront a friend.

In truth, this was a confrontation that was a long time coming and it had so much more to do with than just Malcolm.

As she turned down the block where Monique resided, Serena slowed down as she neared the apartment complex. "What in the . . ." Serena's face shifted from confusion to suspicion.

Malcolm raised his head from the headrest and saw they were parked across from Weequahic Park in front of a three-family apartment building. "What's wrong?" he asked Serena.

When he turned to look over at her, he saw nothing but an empty driver's seat and an open car door. "Aw damn," he swore, reaching over to pull the front door closed before he left the car himself.

He was closing his car door when he looked up the

street and saw something familiar parked at the corner. He did a double take for clarity before he too went dashing into the apartment building behind Serena.

Serena felt like her old "I'm gone knock you out" self as she ate up the stairs with her sneakered feet to reach Monique's second-floor apartment. She had just reached the door when she heard Malcolm's feet echoing in the stairwell behind her.

Serena didn't bother to knock, instead using the spare key Monique gave her ages ago. A little pushy but . . . oh well.

She walked into the apartment like she paid the rent. As a matter of fact, sometimes during the course of their friendship she had. *Ungrateful, no good heifer.*

She strode toward Monique's bedroom. The closer she got the more she could hear the distinctive sounds of sex. The moans. The squeak of bed springs. The knock of the headboard against the wall.

All of it was the sound of a friend's betrayal.

Serena paused and backtracked to the tiny kitchenette. Quietly she reached for an oversized bowl sitting in the dish rack. Barely turning the water on above a trickle, she filled the bowl with cold water. Slowly but surely.

Once full, she grabbed the bowl with both hands and made her way to the bedroom again. Monique let out a rather dramatic squeal of delight.

I got something for your hot behind right here.

The bedroom door was open and Serena casually leaned against the door frame as she watched Zander's ashy buttocks and hips pumping like a piston as he lay atop Monique in the middle of the bed.

Very tongue-in-cheek, Serena stepped into the

room and hoisted the bowl and tossed the water on to them with a splash.

Zander and Monique yelled out in shock and jumped apart, their bodies and the bed drenched with water as they turned to see Serena standing over them. Their faces went from surprise at their impromptu shower to shock at Serena looking down at them with a satisfied smile that didn't reach her eyes.

She took little satisfaction from the guilt clearly written on their faces. She had no words for either of them. Truly, they deserved each other.

"You both know to forget my number, right?"

Malcolm frowned as he reached the doorway and saw the spectacle in front of him. He shook his head and frowned, diverting his eyes from Monique's nakedness.

His took in Zander. "Hope that's not you at your best, dawg?" he asked, laughing when Zander covered his privates with his hands.

Serena arched a brow. "Oh, *that's* his best and as you can see it sure wasn't good enough."

Serena met Monique's eyes and reveled in the fear she saw. She turned to leave.

Zander yanked the sheet from Monique and wrapped it around his waist to jump from the bed and reach out for Serena's wrist. "She threw herself at me, Serena. I don't want her—"

"What?" Monique shrieked.

Serena snatched her arm away from him. "I don't care," she told him with honesty. "And don't touch me again."

Malcolm stepped between them. "Chill out," he ordered in a low, lethal tone.

Zander swung his fist and Malcolm took great pleasure in delivering the man a wicked upper cut that sent him flying back in the air to land spread-eagle in the middle of the bed atop Monique.

They both shouted out as the bed suddenly dropped to the floor.

Serena walked past Malcolm to leave the room, carelessly tossing the bowl aside as she walked out of the apartment. She felt like crying—not because of Zander, but because for the last fourteen years she thought that woman had been her friend—her *sister*.

"I'll drive," Malcolm offered, jogging down the stairs to catch up with her.

Serena nodded, climbing into the passenger seat after handing him the car keys.

"I'm sorry about all of that," he told her, after climbing into the car.

Serena's head fell back against the headrest. "So much has happened in the last twenty-four hours. I just need to get my mind right, you now?" she asked him softly.

Malcolm drove in silence, respecting her wishes. When he finally pulled the car back into the driveway of the house, Malcolm noticed that Serena had fallen asleep.

Not wanting to disturb her sleep and wanting to have her in his arms, Malcolm left the car and came around to lift her easily into his muscled arms. As he carried her into the house that familiar desire to protect her and watch over her welled up in his chest. Not that she needed it, Serena was still one of the strongest women he knew.

Almost any woman he knew would've broken down crying in hysterics at finding her best friend in bed with her ex-boyfriend. Not Serena. He chuckled when he thought of her dashing the two secret lovers with cold water. She handled her business and then left them to waddle in their deceit and the wet sheets. She still had the spunk he admired when they were growing up.

Malcolm looked down at her, resting in his arms, her face even more beautiful in sleep and something he thought was gone tugged at his heart. He carried her into her bedroom and fought the desire to climb into the bed with her and gather her against his body. She felt good in his arms again. Too good.

Chapter 12

Serena was glad that Mondays were her day off. After the night she'd had she didn't roll over in her bed until noon and even then she felt mentally exhausted.

Sex with her ex-husband.

Rehashing the end of her marriage.

Finding out her scandalous best friend had tried to throw Malcolm some rhythm.

Finding out that same scandalous best friend was "involved" with her ex-boyfriend.

But Monique wasn't uppermost in Serena's thoughts. Malcolm was.

Serena rose from the bed, still fully dressed. She began to remove her wrinkled clothing, glad that Malcolm—who she vaguely remembered carrying her to bed—hadn't undressed her himself. He'd seen quite enough of her body yesterday as far as she was concerned.

Naked, she caught a glimpse of her body in the mirror and she paused, tilting her head to the side to study herself. She wasn't mad at what she saw but like any other woman she saw areas for improvement: a stomach that could be a bit flatter, breasts she wished weren't quite so full, hips not so wide.

But none of that had stopped Malcolm's desire. Her eyes glazed over when she remembered how hard his member had been as he filled her with his heat.

No need to ask, "How you like me now?" She already knew the answer. The man wanted her.

And she wanted him as well.

But sex with Malcolm had been easy, or at least easier than dealing with the emotions raging between them. Would she ever completely release her anger about Malcolm walking out on her? Probably not, but was she able to admit that she had been just as unhappy in the marriage and had even considered walking out herself on many occasions? Yes, she could admit that, even if only to herself.

Still, there was a difference. She *thought* about it and Malcolm actually did it.

Serena sighed.

Gathering her things, she threw on her infamous robe and dashed to the bathroom for a long, hot shower that finished waking her up. She had just made her way back to her bedroom, closed the door behind her, and dropped her robe to the floor when there was a soft knock at the door.

"Serena."

She looked over at the closed bedroom door at the sound of her name filtering through it.

Her heart raced.

Covering her breasts with her forearm as if he could see through the door, she called back. "Yes, Malcolm?"

"You finally up?"

She moved her naked frame closer to the door. "Yeah. Why?"

"Open up."

"I'm not dressed."

Thud.

Serena's brows furrowed. "What was that?"

"The thought of you naked got me so hard my other head hit against the door."

Serena actually smiled, but sternly said, "Malcolm."

"Okay . . . all right . . . just kidding."

"What do you want, Malcolm?"

"Come downstairs."

"For what?"

"It's a surprise."

"I'll pass," she told him.

Silence.

Curious and expecting a reply from him, Serena continued to stand by the door.

Still the silence.

She opened the door and peeked out. The hall was empty.

Closing the door back, Serena had to admit that curiosity was definitely killing the cat. She pulled on a man's A-shirt and a pair of sweat shorts that dropped low on her waist. She pulled the door open wide to make her way downstairs barefoot.

She heard noise from the kitchen and headed in that direction. She found Malcolm sitting at the island with an issue of *Vibe* Magazine spread before him as he casually sipped from a mug. The white tee he wore stretched against the breadth of his back and clung to his arms in perfect contrast to the bronze of his skin. Serena had always loved Malcolm's broad shoulders and arms. They were her weak spot.

"I knew you were too nosey not to come down," he mused into his cup before taking a large sip.

True.

Serena's eyes darted around the kitchen but she saw nothing out of the norm.

Malcolm rose, his slippered feet dragging across the tiled floor as he moved. He retrieved a plate from the microwave and set it on the island's top.

Serena's stomach grumbled in protest of its emptiness at the sight of the golden waffles and crisp bacon on the plate.

Now what is he up to, trying to get some more Serena?

Malcolm reclaimed his seat and picked up the magazine. "Just eat it and stop trying to make more out of it than what it is," he said.

"Which is?"

"I made breakfast for myself and decided its just as easy to cook for two as it is for one."

"Thanks." Serena grabbed a glass from the cupboard and moved to the fridge to pour orange juice.

Malcolm just nodded slightly and returned his attention back to his magazine. He finished an article he was reading on a new rapper they were proclaiming was the second coming of Biggie Smalls, and looked up to find Serena with a faraway look in her eyes.

"Serena?"

She blinked and was brought out of her reverie. Her eyes focused as she looked over at Malcolm. "Hmm?"

"What are you thinking about?" he asked as he continued to flip the pages.

Serena ran her tongue along her teeth as she succinctly said, "Slapping Monique silly. No, sillier is more like it."

Malcolm nodded in understanding. "That was low for her to sleep with your ex," he admitted, hating the jealousy he felt burn his gut that Serena was ready to scrap about another man.

"Fight over Zander? *Please.*" Serena took a deep sip

of her juice. "To think she's been in my ear dogging you for years, and I let her come between us sometimes and in the end she was just jealous that I had you and she didn't. That's just too scandalous."

"I never wanted her."

Serena met his eyes. "I know that."

They fell silent as Serena finished her breakfast. "I couldn't pay you to cook when we were married."

"Being a bachelor makes you real handy," he admitted. "I was a boy then, but I'm a man now."

Serena flushed with awareness of just how much man he was and said nothing.

"A lot went down yesterday," he began looking at her over the edge of the magazine.

"That's for sure."

"You okay?" he asked, his concern evident.

"Monique wasn't much of a friend to lose, so they can have each other. Let's see if she likes squeezing on the couch next to his big ole mama for movie night."

Malcolm dropped the magazine. "That's not what I'm talking about now and you know it, Serena."

She purposefully avoided those eyes of his and paid way too much attention to cutting her waffle with the side of her fork.

"Serena."

She dropped the fork and looked up at him in frustration. "It happened, Malcolm, and it will not happen again."

Malcolm's eyes darted down to the way her breasts filled out the T-shirt, the dark outline of her aureoles taunting him. "How can we be so sure?" he asked, his voice deep and as intense as his eyes.

A shiver raced across Serena's skin as her nipples became taut with awareness of him.

Malcolm noticed the two peaks now straining against the thin cotton.

Serena longed for a bra. No, a sweater, definitely the cover of a big, bulky sweater. "I'm positive."

"I'm not."

Serena pressed her thighs together.

"This . . . this chemistry between us isn't going anywhere, Serena," he began, placing his elbows atop the island as he leaned in closer towards her. "You make me just as horny now as you did when we were teenagers dry humping on your aunt's couch."

Serena smiled at the memory. There had been many a make out session on that poor couch. "Whoo-hoo-ee, if that couch could talk," she teased, fanning herself with her hand.

Malcolm laughed. "Tell me about it."

They both fell silent for a moment and got lost in the good old days they shared.

"We've had the belated booty call, Malcolm, what else you want from me?" Serena's voice was soft, just above a whisper.

Malcolm rubbed his chin with his palm as he shook his head slowly. "To be honest. The only thing I know for sure, without question, is that I want you again."

"Wanting and having are two different things."

"You're damn right," Malcolm agreed huskily, rising, his jeans hanging low on his narrow hips as he came to a stop beside her. He used his foot to turn the stool so that he now stood between Serena's knees where she sat. The faint scent of citrus tickled his nose and he inhaled. Malcolm smiled wolfishly as he spread his legs and bent down so the he was eye to eye with her.

Serena's heart pounded furiously and she was absolutely breathless. The man had magnetism that drew her in until her focus was nothing but him. No other man brought out this energy from her soul that begged for her to be claimed by him. And that scared her.

"This is wrong, Malcolm," she whispered softly, even as her eyes locked on his luscious lips.

"Then why does it feel so right?" he asked intensely, before lowering his head to capture her lips with his own.

The first taste of her was an intoxicating blend of the syrup and her lips. Malcolm groaned deep in his throat as he devoured her mouth with his own.

With strength and ease, Malcolm placed his hands on Serena's waist and lifted her from the stool to sit down atop the island. Kicking the stool away, Malcolm stepped closer to Serena and used his arms to press her upper body closer to his.

Serena let her hands trail from Malcolm's elbow and up the arms that made her insides quiver. She gasped lightly as his lips shifted down to kiss a light trail to her neck.

Malcolm found that spot just at the base of her earlobe and was rewarded with a shiver and then a soft hum that resembled a swarm of bees around a honey pot. "Damn it, Serena," he moaned, as the blood rushed to his member, causing it to strain against his zipper.

Feeling desired and sensually playful, Serena backed away from Malcolm, sliding her bottom against the island and swinging her legs up to coyly sit in the middle. If they were going to do *it* again— even if one last time—why not have fun doing it?

"Come back here, girl," Malcolm ordered in husky tones, lightly hitting his palm against the spot she just vacated.

Serena shook her head as she lightly bit her bottom lip and rose to her feet to look down at him. She locked eyes with his as she boldly stripped for him, pulling the T-shirt over her head to toss onto his head.

Malcolm shook it off, not wanting to miss the show.

Serena felt powerful as Malcolm's mouth gaped open and his eyes darkened a shade further as she wiggled her shorts down her hips and legs to kick away with her feet. Naked, bronzed, and bold, she stood on display for him. She had Malcolm eating out of the palm of her hand and that felt *soooo* good.

She climbed down from the island and walked out the kitchen.

Malcolm watched Serena, intoxicated with want as she stopped in the doorway of the kitchen to turn and beckon him to follow with a bend of her finger.

Wanting to play as well, Malcolm quickly shed his clothing. Serena made it as far as the bottom of the staircase. He prowled behind her and used one strong arm around her waist to lightly jerk her back against his body. His rod perfectly snuggled up between her buttocks as he shifted his hand up from her hip to firmly cup one velvety, chocolate breast.

Serena shivered with a moan, letting her eyes drift closed as Malcolm walked them forward to press the front of her body into the wall. She gasped at the cool feel against her nipples and thighs as the heat of Malcolm's body sandwiched her from behind.

Malcolm's pressure was slight so Serena used her bottom to push back against him for just enough room to turn around and face him with her hair now splayed against the wall. She let her hands trace the hard, well-defined contours of his shoulders.

"Kiss me," she breathed huskily, her eyes dropping from his eyes to his lips.

With a sinful grin, Malcolm lowered his head and did just that, with a fierceness that made Serena glad for the support of both the wall and the man as her knees went weak.

Malcolm bent his legs, lowering himself to capture one of her breasts in his mouth. He circled the tight bud with skill before sucking it and then moving across to the other to continue his feast.

"Malcolm," she sighed in sweet pleasure.

He bent his knees further, until he was almost squatting with his legs wide apart to lick a hot and steady trail down the valley of her breasts to eventually circle her navel. He felt her shuddering in response to him and he reveled in it.

"Hold on," he warned, looking up at her as he lifted her up slightly to place each of her legs on his shoulders.

Serena pressed her back to the wall as he positioned his mouth right at the swollen lips of her core exposed to him. And at that first feel of his tongue on her bud, Serena didn't care if she fell as she shifted her hands from her knees to grasp her own breasts.

"Hmm."

Malcolm deepened the sucking motion until nearly all of her core filled his eager mouth.

"Hmmm." Serena felt that familiar tingling warmth in her toes and Malcolm worked her spot with true dedication. A fine sheen of perspiration coated her body.

Malcolm inhaled deeply of her unique womanly scent and enjoyed the taste of her as her lips suctioned his mouth. He wondered how he lived all these years without being able to roll over in bed and indulge in her whenever he wanted.

Breaking the intimate kiss, Malcolm came up for air, leaning his head back to look up at her. He was enthralled by how uninhibited she was as she teased her own nipples with nimble fingers.

Coming down from a physical high, Serena's chest

heaved with each haggard breath as she struggled for control. She swung her leg over Malcolm's head and stood on her own two feet.

Malcolm looked confused and turned his head to see Serena's delicious bottom as she jogged up the stairs. He watched as she reached the top and sat on the top step, again beckoning him with that finger.

Malcolm unbent his legs as he looked up at her. This sexy and mischievous Serena was the lover he remembered well and it made him want her more. He climbed the stairs two at a time, anxious now to bury himself deep within her until her smiles and joking were gone as she faced some very serious loving.

Serena held a hand out to Malcolm's chest just as he stood one step below her, leaving him directly between her legs with his curved member level with her mouth.

She cocked her head to the side and looked up at him, leaning in slightly.

Malcolm's heart nearly flew up into his throat. "Don't tease—"

She took him into her mouth, closing her eyes with a delicious moan as she enjoyed the feel of his hardness against her lips and clever tongue.

Malcolm reached his hand out to cup the back of Serena's head, praying his knees didn't give out and send him flying backward down the stairs. Just when he felt he was going to pass out, Serena released him with one final kiss to the throbbing tip.

Malcolm uncrossed his eyes and shook his head as he struggled for clarity. "Damn," he swore, reaching out for the banister.

When his eyes focused, Serena was strutting to his bedroom, turning at the door to beckon him once again. She then disappeared into the room with a wink. Serena was driving him wild and Malcolm was sure that he would follow this temptress to the bowels of hells to have her.

Serena decided on Malcolm's room because she knew he had condoms. In the room, she grabbed one of Malcolm's silk ties and draped it around her slender neck as she moved to stand behind the padded chair in front of his desk.

Her eyes devoured the sight of him naked and aroused, sculpted and lean as his erection led him into the room. He stopped at his dresser and removed a condom from the top drawer, sheathing himself with the latex.

"Sit down," she ordered huskily, bending over the back to pat the seat of the chair.

"What are you trying to do to me?" he asked as he moved toward her, the muscles of his chocolate body flexing with every movement.

"The same thing you're doing to me, Malcolm Saint James. Turning me on," she answered.

He sat in the chair and Serena came around to straddle his lap. She brought her hands up and lightly grasped his face as his hands caressed her waist.

Their eyes locked and held.

Suddenly everything between them changed.

Serena fully took in the magnitude of it all. This handsome and masculine and virile and sexy man was not just any man. This was Malcolm. Her Malcolm. Her first love. Her first lover. Once her husband. A man she had loved with every fiber of her being. A man she had almost hated just as much. A man she thought she would never have in her arms again. But here he was. And although she thought whatever natural link they shared from that first childhood meeting was irrevocably broken, being with him felt *right*.

Malcolm looked up into Serena's face and it was a face he knew so well. A face he had seen change and grow over the years since they first met that summer day all those years ago. A face he had loved to stare at while she slept, kiss for any and every reason, and stroke just for the hell of it. This was the face of a woman that he once loved, but also the face of a woman who once hurt him deeply. Deeper than he had ever admitted to anyone, maybe even himself. But as he looked up into her face, caressing every nuance with his eager eyes, he was overwhelmed by how much he missed it.

Slowly they kissed and both were shook by the intensity.

There was a constant wave of electricity and awareness between them. A heat created by the unique combination of this man and this particular woman: Malcolm and Serena Saint James.

Serena felt afraid of the emotions that were bubbling between them and wanted to reclaim the playful momentum. "Put your hands behind your back," she told him as she lightly bit his bottom lip, removing his tie from around her as he did.

She reached behind him and tied his wrists lightly behind the chair. "Do you remember the time we made love on the balcony in the rain?" she asked, as she guided his head to her breasts.

"How could I forget?"

She reached between them to stroke the full throbbing length of him as she arched her back and offered her breast to him. Serena smiled and sighed as Malcolm took one ripe tip into his mouth with a low hungry growl from deep in his throat.

Moist with anticipation and eager to have him, Serena placed both her feet down on the floor and rose up on her toes to guide herself down onto Malcolm's hardness slowly, inch by delicious inch until she fit him snugly and completely.

"Serena," Malcolm groaned, falling forward to rest his forehead in the sweet valley between her breasts.

Serena entwined her fingers against his nape and leaned back as far as her outstretched arms would allow to begin a slow and rhythmic pop of her hips as she rode Malcolm like there was nothing else in the world she wanted to do.

Malcolm's hands itched to caress her and he felt himself tugging at the binds at his wrists to be free to stroke that warm, moist spot between her thighs and feel the bounce of her buttocks as she worked her walls against the length of him with wicked ease.

Serena gave in to her pleasure, abandoning any shyness or inhibitions as she let herself ride the high of riding Malcolm.

No words were spoken. None were needed. They were in tune to each other, both wanting to please and be pleased. Lost in the desire, seeking the enjoyment, wanting the climax.

As she felt that familiar tingling of her toes, Serena brought herself closer to Malcolm, using one hand to lift a full breast to guide to Malcolm's gaping mouth. He obliged and she shivered as her heart hammered. She quickened the pace of her hips as her bud swelled and met his hardness.

Malcolm deepened his sucking motions as he felt that tremble of Serena's walls against him. He knew she was near her release and he firmly planted his feet on the floor and began to work his hips upward to meet each of her strokes deeply.

Serena cried out hoarsely, arching her back, and clutching Malcolm's strong upper arms as swells of pleasure controlled her body as she came.

Malcolm's arousal was intensified by the sounds of Serena as her groan lowered into that hum he craved to create and the feel of her walls clutching and releasing his tool rhythmically. He winced with a grunt as he came as well.

Serena clutched him tightly to her, trembling with her release as she continued to work her hips to draw the last of Malcolm's release from his body until he was limp.

Their ragged breathing and rapid heartbeats seemed to echo against the walls of the room.

"We can't keep doing this," Serena gasped.

"I know," Malcolm agreed, out of breath.

They slumped against each other.

The doorbell rang suddenly and Serena jumped up in alarm. They had just been in a world alone and now the intrusion of the doorbell set her heart to racing all over again. She looked around, a little disoriented as she wiped her face with her hands.

"Serena," Malcolm called to her. "It's the doorbell."

"Huh?" she asked breathily.

"The doorbell, baby, it's just the doorbell," he told her calmly.

Serena nodded, still a little out of sorts. She left Malcolm's bedroom, closing the door behind her before she dashed into her room to rush into a pair of old jeans and a T-shirt. She jogged down the stairs.

"Serena!" Malcolm called out.

She was already at the bottom opening the door. She smiled at the sight of Luther and Elaine. "Hi newlyweds. Come in, come in," she said, stepping back to pull the door open wide to let them in from the bitter cold.

Luther took in Serena's wild hair and glassy eyes. "Where's that boy of mine?" he asked, his big voice booming. "We brought ya'll some gifts from Jamaica."

Serena's mouth shaped into an "O" as she remembered just how she left Malcolm upstairs. "He's in his room—"

Luther turned for the stairs. "I'll go get him—"

"No!" Serena shouted out in alarm, causing Luther to jerk back. She smiled at them as they looked at her like she was from Mars. "I'm going up anyway and . . . um . . . I'll tell him to come down. Ya'll . . . uh . . . have a seat in the den and he'll be right down."

"Okay," Elaine said gently, taking Luther's arm to guide him into the next room.

Serena threw another big smile before she turned and flew up the stairs and into Malcolm's room, closing the door securely behind her.

There he sat, naked and patiently waiting, his member now limp between his strong thighs.

"I'm so sorry," Serena gushed, moving behind him to release his wrists.

He nodded his gleaming bald head. "I wondered just how long I would have to sit here," he said, massaging his wrists as he rose from the chair.

"Your Dad and Elaine are downstairs," Serena told him, covering her lips with her hand as she struggled not to laugh.

She failed, swallowing it back with a snort.

Malcolm turned and looked at her with a cocked brow.

She bit her bottom lip.

Luther walked into the kitchen to fix himself a cup of coffee and immediately saw the discarded clothing. His eyes shifted up as if he could see through the ceiling at just what his son and ex-daughter-in-law were up to upstairs.

Chuckling, he didn't go in any further and turned on his heel to leave the kitchen. Sticking his head into the den, he said to his wife, "Come on, baby, let's go."

Elaine turned on the sofa to look a him in confusion. "Why are we leaving? We just got here."

"I think we're interrupting," he told her, with a nod of his head upstairs.

"Oh," she said, her face a mirror of understanding. She picked up the shopping bag holding the gifts and rose.

They had pulled on their overcoats when Malcolm came jogging down the stairs with his laptop tucked under his arm. "Ya'll leaving?" he asked, frowning.

Luther and Elaine shared a brief look before turning back to face Malcolm.

"Yeah, we're gone head on home," Luther told him.

Serena came down the stairs next. "Are you leaving? You just got here. I wanted to hear all about Jamaica."

"We don't want to interrupt," Elaine said lightly.

Malcolm and Serena looked at each other, laughing nervously. "What do you mean interrupt? Interrupt what? You're not interrupting anything. Right Serena, they're not interrupting, right?"

"No, sure ain't," Serena chirped in, sliding her hands into her back pockets.

Luther looked at them both in obvious amusement before he began to shrug out of his coat with another chuckle.

Serena took their coats and hung them back up in their foyer closet, joining everyone in the den. But not before she dashed into the kitchen and scooped up their discarded clothing to hide in a lower cupboard.

In the den, Malcolm hooked his computer up to the TV just as Serena curled on the love seat. That empty spot beside her never looked more inviting. Grabbing the remote, he gave in to the urge to be near her and slid on the seat beside her.

The move surprised Serena, especially as Luther

and Elaine looked at them in open curiosity. Avoiding their eyes, Serena focused on the television.

As the montage of the wedding played with Etta James' soulful blues classic "At Last" playing softly in the background, they all laughed or were touched by scenes from the wedding and reception.

Malcolm's heart swelled at the clip of Serena and him dancing together and his hands sought and found a comfortable spot on her thigh.

Wow, Serena thought, seeing that shot of them for the first time.

"That's a beautiful shot of you together," Elaine sighed, entwining her fingers with Luther's.

"Sure is," Luther agreed.

Serena and Malcolm looked comfortable with each other, aware of each other, in love with each other.

Serena stood suddenly. "I'm thirsty. Anyone else want something to drink?" she said, her voice anxiously high and almost shrieking.

Before anyone could even answer her question, Serena was out of the room faster than a speeding bullet. She headed for the kitchen and leaned heavily over the sink as she turned on the faucet and splashed her neck and face with cold water. She felt like she was about to have a panic attack and she focused on inhaling and exhaling deeply and slowly.

What in the devil's drawers was going on between her and Malcolm? What were they doing? Were they crazy?

The fine hairs on the back of her neck stood on end and Serena *knew* Malcolm was behind her.

"You okay?" he asked, just before those incredibly skillful hands landed softly on her forearm.

See, like that. Why is it that only this man can touch me and turn my knees to jelly and set my heart racing faster than a NASCAR race car?

"Serena?" he asked again with concern, turning her to face him.

Quickly she forced a smile to her lips and was immediately overwhelmed by his handsome, keen features.

I'm not crazy, this isn't just lust, this isn't just sex, it's manifesting itself in the form of lust and sex but this is much more and it's scaring the shit out of me, she thought, even as she kept on that phony smile.

Malcolm's eyes darted about her face as he studied her. She looked like an animal staring down the barrel of a hunter's gun. "What's wrong?" he asked, raising his hand to lightly grasp her chin and tilt her face upwards.

Now was not the time nor place to discuss how crazy they were for playing with fire.

"Nothing," Serena lied and then moved past him to walk out of the kitchen. "I'm gonna go up and lie down. I'm not feeling so good. Please give Luther and Elaine my regrets."

Malcolm turned and his eyes followed her retreat.

Chapter 13

"Ninety-nine . . . one hundred. . . ."

Malcolm paused in his push-ups, liking the physical exertion as he tried to think through his problems. And because his problems were big—gargantuan even—he began his tenth set of one hundred push-ups right in the middle of the den.

Malcolm had loved Serena since before he knew what secrets girls held under their skirts. He loved her as a friend, a girlfriend, and then a wife. He was slowly discovering that he was now falling back in love with her as his ex-wife.

Did he believe those deep feelings came to him in one month for a woman he just met? No, but this wasn't just any woman, this was Serena. He saw a lot of the same traits he first cherished as a friend still there. She was loyal. Feisty. Funny. Strong. Courageous. Independent.

And traits from her as a girlfriend. She was caring. Supportive. Attractive.

And traits from her as wife because there was no denying that she was still the sexy woman he married times a thousand.

But there were other things about her that developed

over the years they were apart. She was more focused. Goal oriented. Confident. Ambitious.

Those were things he found sexy and alluring in a woman as he entered his late twenties and thirties. With age Serena had become the woman he had always wanted in the first place.

"Fifty . . . fifty-one . . . fifty-two," he continued, counting aloud as he pushed himself further.

But . . .

Even though he recognized his feelings, did he want to pursue them?

"Sixty-one . . . sixty-two—"

Ding-dong.

He paused midway down on a push-up and instinctively looked toward the foyer.

Rising from the floor he grabbed his T-shirt and pulled it over his head as he walked to the door.

"Hey Hamp," he said, smiling at the older man. "Come in out of that cold."

"Hi Malcolm. How are you?" Hamp asked as he unbuttoned his wool overcoat.

"Good, good. You?"

"I'm making it. Is Serena here?" Hamp asked, as Malcolm hung up his coat.

"She's upstairs."

"Go up and get her for me and then ya'll meet me in the den, okay?"

"Sure," Malcolm agreed, curious as to what his grandmother had in store for them now.

He jogged up the stairs to knock on Serena's door.

Serena looked up from the interior design magazines she was browsing through. She was hoping not to see Malcolm again tonight. She had a lot on her mind and he was a major distraction.

"Come in," she called out.

The door opened slowly and Malcolm filled her doorway. "Hey."

"What's up?" she asked.

"Hamp wants to see us both downstairs," he said, noticing that she must have showered because she had changed clothes.

Serena closed her magazine. *Now what?* she wondered as she rolled off the bed.

"Hey, about today," Malcolm began.

Serena paused to look up at him as they both filled the doorway. "Yes, Malcolm?"

"We need to talk about what's going on between us."

Serena's pulse raced. "And exactly what's going on?" she asked, her eyes dropping to study and long for his lips.

"Hell if I know, Serena," he replied with frustration.

"Well, when you know fill me in," she told him over her shoulder as she headed for the stairs.

"Olivia wanted me to give these to you," Hamp said, handing first Malcolm and then Serena a small manila envelope.

They looked at each other from where they sat opposite each other in the den clutching envelopes that were scented faintly with *White Diamonds* perfume.

"She asked that neither of you discuss what's in those letters with anyone."

Malcolm looked down at the envelope in his hand and smiled a little at his grandmother's slanted handwriting. It was barely legible but it was distinctly hers. Sadness flooded him, but curiosity at his grandmother's craftiness filled him as well.

Serena set her envelope down on the coffee table and then wiped her suddenly sweaty palms on the legs of her jeans.

"I'll being going now," Hamp said, rising.

Serena rose, seeing that Malcolm was deep in thought. "I'll walk you out, Hamp," she offered, following him to the foyer.

She returned moments later to find Malcolm still on the couch, his head in his hands, his shoulders slumped. It was a sad sight that tugged at her heart.

"You know when Auntie died I thought a time would never come when I could think of her and not cry," Serena said softly, moving across the room to sit beside him and wrap her arm around his shoulders. "And it took some time but mostly when I think of her I'm laughing at something funny she said or did. Or I'm remembering something wise that she taught me growing up."

Malcolm raised his head and although sadness filled his eyes, he kept the tears from falling.

"And I remember a good friend of mine told me that now I have my very own angel in heaven looking down at me. Now so do you."

Malcolm smiled a bit, remembering speaking those very words to Serena the night her aunt passed on. "It was nice back then when I had your back and you had mine," he said.

Serena nodded in agreement. "You okay?" she asked softly, as she rubbed light circles on his back.

"I miss her a lot," he revealed in a voice that was tinged with his pain. "She was my biggest supporter but also the first one to tell me when I was wrong. If it wasn't for her I wouldn't have gone to film school. I wouldn't be who I am today."

"I remember you always, *always* had a camera around that little skinny neck when we were growing up," Serena teased. "It's cool to see you accomplish those dreams we used to lie in the park and talk about. Mister Emmy-Winning Filmmaker."

Malcolm looked bashful, but he was proud of his accomplishments. "I'm really excited about the one I'm working on now. You know how much I love hip-hop culture."

Serena rolled her eyes playfully. "Do I ever."

"And next month I'll be sitting in a room, interviewing these people. And it runs the full history of rap and hip-hop from the Sugarhill Gang to Dana Dane, Slick Rick, & Dougie Fresh to the top dogs of today like Jay-Z and Nas, Fat Joe and Fifty Cent. *Me*, you know, I'm doing this. These guys are opening up their homes, their lives, their histories . . . for *me*."

Serena was touched by how excited he was. "Well, if you ask me it's just as big a deal for them to meet you as it is for you to meet them."

"Thanks. That's not true, but I thank you anyway," he told her, reaching over to muss her hair like he did when they were twelve.

"I'm proud of you," she said with honesty as she met his eyes. "And so is Mama James."

There was that hum of electricity between them. That chemistry that had nothing at all to do with sex but everything in the world to do with their growing awareness and re-emerging feelings for each other.

"I know your aunt is proud of you too, about to do your business thang," he smiled, knocking his knee against hers.

"Yeah, I am," she said, as if finally realizing that her dreams were about to be fulfilled. "It's a little scary but I really think I can do it, you know? I found this awesome location. The owner is just moving her business to New York and she wants to lease out the spot and all the equipment. She's even agreed to wait to do the lease until after all of this is done and I have the money. Although the place is a little larger than I wanted and a lot more expensive, I've decided what the hell I'll go for it. I'm already looking for new beauticians straight out of school to rent a couple booths and just . . . just working it all out, doing my thing. I really think Auntie is looking out for me and steering me in the right direction."

"So whenever I'm in town I can get my shave on right?" he asked, rubbing his large hand over his gleaming bald head.

"No doubt, no doubt," she told him, looking away first, unable to take how it saddened her to remember that Malcolm would be going back to his life in New York.

Malcolm felt a loss when Serena moved her hand from his back. Just a simple and innocent touch from her gave him actual goose bumps.

"So what are you going to do with the house after we move back out?" she asked lightly, looking around the den where Mama James' presence was prominent.

Malcolm rose and walked over to the large photo of his grandmother hanging over the fireplace. He shrugged. "I don't know. Maybe rent it out? I know I can't sell it, but I don't exactly want strangers all up in my grandmother's house either."

"So you wouldn't ever move back to Newark?" Serena asked, and then hated herself for caring.

Malcolm turned to look over at her. "For the right reasons I would," he told her, purposefully locking his eyes with hers.

Serena's heart raced and again she asked herself: *What are we doing?* The days of Serena & Malcolm were over and there was no going back.

"So, um, we've been avoiding these letters here for long enough," she said, hoping to divert those deep-set eyes away from her.

"Yup, we have," he agreed.

"I think I'm going to take mine upstairs and leave

you alone to read yours," Serena offered, picking up her envelope from the table and rising from the sofa. "Okay?"

He nodded, wiping his hand over his mouth as he walked over to reclaim his seat on the sofa. "Okay."

Long after Serena was gone, Malcolm sat with his chin in his hands as he stared at the envelope and wondered just what Mama James had in store for them next.

Serena kicked off her slippers and climbed into the middle of her unmade bed to read the letter.

Dearest Serena,

Of course if you are reading this then I have gone on to heaven (I hope) and you have accepted my challenge to move into my home with our Malcolm. Please beg an old woman's pardon for trying a little matchmaking and know that I meant well. But let's face it, you two are so stubborn and so willful that I knew it would take something so drastic to get you in the same vicinity. And by now I hope you two have at least stopped fighting like cats and dogs.

I don't know if you know this but I always admired that you two were bold enough to cross that line from friends to much more than friends. To take a chance on losing everything to win everything. I wish I had the same faith in myself . . .

Serena arched a brow at that line. Was Mama James about to drop some gossip? Serena hurried to the next page.

I shall tell you something I have never revealed to another soul and maybe you both will understand why

I am fighting so hard for the two of you. I have been in love with my dear friend Hamp for over three decades.

Serena gasped dramatically at that. "Well, you go Olivia, girl," she cheered.

And never once in all those years did I reveal my feelings to him. He still does not know and you must never tell him.

"Oh," Serena sighed, thinking it sad that Mama James lived with her secret love for Hamp all those years and now she was gone and he would never know. Did Hamp love her as well?

You both had the courage that I didn't have to admit to loving your friend and I say don't waste it. Your problems were nothing age, maturity, and a shortening of the distance between you couldn't fix. You both had so much love for each other and I refuse to believe that all of that love has just vanished. All I ask is that you try, take a good look at the man Malcolm is and not continue to hold it against him because of the actions of the boy that he was. You took a chance on love before and I say don't be afraid to take that chance again. Regardless, I will always think of you as my granddaughter and look over you from heaven right along with Vanessa.

Olivia

"Wow," Serena said in low voice. Serena felt a chill race over her body.

Mama James had tapped right into the fear Serena was feeling. She took a chance on falling in love with

Malcolm before and she'd wound up with a broken heart. Could she trust him again with her heart?

She could sense those feelings resurfacing for him and so she guessed the real question was, did she have a choice?

Malcolm stood outside Serena's bedroom door, his grandmother's letter in his hand as he wrestled with it all. He wanted to walk in there, grab Serena and make sweet, passionate love to her until they both were breathless.

But he didn't.

He continued on to his bedroom, closing the door behind him. Bathing the room with light, he sat down on the edge of the bed and read his grandmother's letter for the third time:

My Beloved Malcolm:

Is it even necessary for me to say that I miss you? And I know you miss me as well. I hope you're not too mad at this old lady for making you work a little for your inheritance. But we both know this has nothing to do with that house—although you better take good care of it, and you better not sell it, and you better not rent it to some couple with five crumb snatchers to move in and tear it up—but I digress. This is about you and Serena waking up to smell the coffee or whatever else necessary to make sure that you both finish those dreams you had of having your own family and building a life together. I passed on a chance to have that kind of love with Hamp, that would be built on a good, solid friendship and I would hate to see you waste the chance that you took. Just wanted you both to give it an honest try and if I had to get you two under one roof any way that I could, I did.

*You know you love her, so stop being so stubborn.
Follow your heart, grandson, and it won't lead you
wrong. You both have already wasted so many years
apart. Are you going to waste any more time?*

*Anyway I'm on the other side now and I'm now
looking down on you with pride. You are a good
grandson, and a good man, Malcolm Saint James.
And I'll love you always.*

Mama

Malcolm closed the letter and set it on his night-stand. He turned off the light, stripped naked and lay on his bed with his hands behind his head. He had to work out his thoughts and the silence of the bedroom was the perfect backdrop.

He was feeling deep emotions for Serena again and Lord knows he wanted her so badly that just the thought of her made him harder than steel, but did he want to get involved with her again? Did he want to take a chance with his heart? Serena wasn't the only one hurt by their break-up.

Had the wounds healed enough for them to build a new life together?

Follow your heart, grandson.

Malcolm lay there for hours well into the night, weighing the pros and cons.

The only thing he knew for sure after his long deliberations was that he wanted Serena in his arms, in his bed, and his life. To hell with the cons.

Rising, he grabbed a sheet to wrap around his waist and made his way to her bedroom. He didn't even bother to knock as his heart hammered in his chest. He dropped the sheet and lifted the covers to climb in bed next to her, gathering her into his arms.

She stirred in her sleep, stretching her body against

him. "Malcolm?" she asked, turning over in the darkness onto her back.

Malcolm lowered his head and captured her lips in a heated kiss. "Serena," he whispered fiercely against her mouth.

As the kiss deepened, Malcolm removed Serena's pajama bottoms and felt a surge of desire when she lifted her hips in welcome of his seduction. Her top followed next and he pulled her naked form close to his, just enjoying the blended heat and softness of her body.

Malcolm positioned himself above Serena and worshipped her body with his hands and lips from her slender neck to her full breasts, the plum of womanhood, and the long length of her legs. Serena lay back on the bed, her arms and legs opened wide as she enjoyed every sensual moment of it. It was slow yet deliberate. Tender yet fierce, as his words of her beauty whispered against her skin hotly.

When he lay atop her, his throbbing erection pressing into her belly, she sighed, letting her own hands caress every inch of his strong back and buttocks with ease. She entwined her legs with his and purred deliciously as he blessed her with tiny kisses upon her neck.

The energy between them tonight was a thousand times more intense as they worshipped each others bodies and reveled in the pleasure that it seemed only they could give to each other.

This was not sex. This was beyond a physical mating. This was quite simply making love. That connection between two people who knew they were made for each other. Every moan, every sigh, every stroke, every kiss, every lock of the eyes, and every beating of the heart in unison was a testimony of their emotions. Emotions that neither could deny.

Malcolm sheathed himself and entered her slowly, holding her arms above her head with their hands entwined and their eyes locked as he filled her completely. He kissed her, swallowing her gasp of pure pleasure as he began to slowly circle his hips, his strong muscular buttocks flexing and releasing as he tried to touch his maleness to every nook and cranny of her femininity.

Serena was touched by his intensity. She was caught up in the passion. And she was blown away by the emotions so clearly spelled out in his eyes. She bit her bottom lip to keep from whispering how much she loved him still. And was surprised when Malcolm lowered his head to her neck and kissed a trail to her earlobe where he suckled her gently and said with a fierceness that made her tremble, "God, I love you, Serena. I've always loved you. I never stopped."

Serena couldn't stop the tears that welled up in her eyes as Malcolm continued that slow, soulful, grind.

"Don't cry, baby," he pleaded, as he kissed the tracks of her tears and released her hands to wrap his strong arms around her tightly as that wickedly good grind continued.

Serena buried her face into his neck and wrapped her arms around him as well as they both began to shiver with the first waves of their release. And they came together for what seemed an eternity, spiraling together in a world where no one existed or mattered but them. They clutched each other tightly and gave in to the white hot spasms of their release.

Serena stroked Malcolm's back as he lay on his stomach beside her. She couldn't sleep. Her thoughts were heavy.

Malcolm said he loves me, she thought as she let her

fingers trail from his buttocks up to his shoulder as he snored lightly.

And yes, she loved him as well.

But she had already decided that she just couldn't take the chance again with her heart. They had the love and friendship before and they ended up divorcing and hating—or at least pretending to hate—each other for nearly a decade.

They had gotten past the past and agreed they'd both made mistakes. They were back on good terms. His life was set in New York and she was about to start her new business in New Jersey. They both had their own lives and had been doing just fine without each other for the last ten years. They had just another three weeks in the house together. Why tempt fate? Why not leave well enough alone?

Chapter 14

Serena was up, out of bed, showered, dressed, and headed to work before Malcolm could even think about rolling over. She tried her best to focus on work and not the heated lovemaking she shared with Malcolm the night before. She would deal with Malcolm when she got back to the house.

There were plenty of things she could focus on besides him. Like sitting Donald and Evelyn down to tell them she was leaving soon to start her own salon. Or making time today to go by the cosmetology school downtown to scout for new beauticians. Or getting estimates on insurance. Her business license application that still needed to be completed. Finding a contractor to do the minor work inside the shop to get it just the way she wanted.

Serena pulled her long, auburn weave up into a ponytail to get the hair off her neck as she motioned for her next client to sit in her chair. Already knowing the woman wanted a touch-up and cut, Serena starting parting her shoulder length hair into four sections as she chatted with her and the waiting clients about the soap operas.

She was smoothing her client's permed new growth

with her gloved fingers when the bell over the door rang. As did everyone else's, Serena's eyes darted to the front of the shop. And those eyes went cold and hostile at the sight of Monique entering.

"Dee Dee," Serena called out to the new shampoo girl, not once taking her eyes off her former friend. "Will you wash Mrs. Ripton for me and give her a deep conditioner, please?"

As soon as the eighteen-year-old shampoo girl led her client away, Serena headed for Monique. "Outside," Serena snapped low enough just for Monique's ears as she breezed past her and walked the short distance away from the shop to the parking lot.

She didn't even feel the cold she was so pissed off. As soon as Monique joined her outside, Serena whirled on her. "What in the hell are you doing here?" she said nastily.

Monique pointed to her head. "I came to get my hair done," she said simply, like there was no beef between them.

"Are you crazy or are you on something stronger than all that weed you smoke?" Serena asked. "Stay the hell away from me, Monique. That's the best thing for you to do."

Serena cast her a meaningful stare that was filled with clear warning and walked past her to go back to the shop.

"Why you tripping over some dude you ain't want anyway?" Monique yelled behind her. "You gone let him come between us?"

Serena froze in her steps and then turned back to march over to Monique and stand nose to nose with her. "Did you throw yourself at Malcolm?" she asked, her voice steely.

Monique stepped back from the anger in Serena's eyes. "Malcolm? Don't you mean Zander?"

Serena pointed her finger in Monique's face, nudging her as she said, "I couldn't care less about you, Zander, his small penis or his big mama."

Monique frowned. "Don't nobody want no dang on Malcolm but you."

"You know, why am I even out here arguing in the snow with you? It don't matter because you never have been a real friend to me anyway. You're negative, you're jealous, you're a hater—"

"Jealous?" Monique said with attitude and disbelief.

"Damn right, because you ain't squat and you're never gonna be squat."

"You know what Serena? You crazy. What you got that I want?"

"Way too much for me to have the time to run it down for you, that's for sure. Just stay away from me, Monique."

Monique rolled her eyes and sucked her teeth with a "Whatever."

Serena turned and walked back to the salon. She looked over her shoulder and saw Monique headed back to her car. Before she could talk herself out of it, Serena scooped up a handful of snow and made a loose ball with it. "Hey Monique," she called, even as she took aim.

Monique turned and the snow hit her full in the face, catching her off guard and knocking her backward into the snow.

Laughing, Serena wiped her hands on her jeans and went back to the shop feeling a whole lot better.

Malcolm was disappointed when he woke up and nothing but Serena's unique citrus scent was left in the bed. Smiling at the night they shared, he had showered and dressed in a charcoal-gray sweater and cords for his trip into New York.

He and his team had their production meeting at his loft apartment and because it was a lot easier for Mohammed to go the mountain, he made the trip back home.

After everyone was gone, Malcolm walked around his loft and was surprised to find it cold to him. The masculine contemporary design spoke of his bachelor status. There was no way a woman would feel comfortable in this space and children were a definite no-no with all the sharp, angular edges and glass surfaces.

And he realized as he walked over to the far end that served as his bedroom, that he wanted his life filled with a woman—one particular woman—and children.

As he thought of Serena and his grandmother's house back in Newark, he wasn't quite as anxious to return to his detached New York living.

He spent the rest of the day going over his production notes and making some phones calls to firm up interview dates. He even worked out a bit on his treadmill and lifted some weights, basically trying to waste time until he thought Serena would be home.

Home.

Yes, when he thought of home he thought of Serena and he thought of that house where he grew up, definitely not his current surroundings.

Sweaty from his workout, Malcolm took a shower, changed into a sweat suit and grabbed his keys to leave the loft and head back to Jersey. He couldn't wait to get there.

Serena stalled on going back to the house as long as she could, even taking two walk-ins at 4:30 P.M.—something that was usually a no-no for her.

When she did enter the house through the kitchen, Malcolm was at the stove stirring in a pot. "Hey what's up," he greeted her with a big toothy grin that melted her heart.

"Hi. Whatcha cooking?" she asked, pulling her satchel over her head to set on the island along with her keys.

"Beef stew," he said, turning to lean his hard buttocks against the counter's edge as he crossed his arms over his chest. "Want some?"

"I don't think we should get involved again," Serena blurted out in one rushed breath.

Malcolm crossed one foot over his ankle and nodded as he looked down at his feet briefly, before looking back up at her with a cool expression. "Fine," he said shortly, before turning back to his stew without another word.

Serena's face was confused. "Is that all you have to say?" she asked, astonished.

Malcolm looked over his shoulder at her. "Yeah."

Serena stomped her foot. "Last night you were making love to me and telling me over and over you never stopped loving me—"

"That's still true, Serena," he said simply.

Serena opened her mouth to say something but could form no words. She felt like acting a straight fool and flinging her bag at his arrogant head but she didn't. What was her problem? She told the man she didn't want any involvement and he agreed.

"No more sex either," she told him.

Malcolm breathed heavily as he turned to again lean his buttocks against the counter and face her. "What do you want me to do, Serena, beg you? Well, I'm not going to. I want you and if you give me half the chance I'll knock your boots from here to Sunday. But I ain't begging you for it."

Serena met his cool eyes and picked up her things and left the kitchen, fighting the urge to stomp up the stairs. "That arrogant, big-headed, stubborn, crusty foot—"

She struggled for more insults as she closed her bedroom door and locked it. "What kinda love is that?" she complained.

"Fine," she said, imitating his coolness.

"Liar, doesn't know what love is and never did. You *fight* for love," she yelled at the door as she fell back against the bed and covered her head with her pillows to scream with frustration.

Malcolm dropped his spoon into the sink and turned the gas fire off under the pot. Three more weeks and that woman and her craziness would be out of his hair—well, if he had any hair.

Just last night she was crying and telling him she loved him as well.

Malcolm paused as he walked out of the kitchen. Actually, when he made his heartfelt declaration last night, Serena *hadn't* said the words in return.

Serena didn't love him?

He couldn't believe that. Call it bravado, arrogance, or just pure belief in himself as a man, but he knew Serena had feelings for him. He hadn't been alone in that bed last night.

But that was sex and sex was not always love.

Hell, her tears didn't exactly mean anything. He made love to women before and they'd shed tears, and he sure wasn't fool enough to believe every one of them had been in love.

He had been so caught up in his own feelings that he had yet to pause and ponder that Serena didn't feel the same way. Here he was making plans for their future when she was working up the nerve to tell him to back off.

Well, if that's what she wanted then to hell with it, that was exactly what she was going to get.

That coolness between them returned during their final weeks in the house. Oh, they spoke and even shared their meals, but they both ignored that electricity humming between them as they focused on everything but each other.

And although neither would admit it, they both were absolutely miserable.

Serena still spent most of her time in her room and she noticed that Malcolm was spending more and more of his days in New York, coming back to the house so late that sometimes she was already in bed. She hated the jealousy that claimed her as she pictured him carousing with girlfriends—old or new. But what could she say, she ignored Mama James' advice to give their love a second chance and overruled her heart with her head and her fears of being hurt again.

She went through hell with gasoline drawers ten years ago. For goodness sake, the man walked out on her and left their marriage, who wouldn't be hesitant to give him a chance to do it again?

So with three days left until they were both free to go back to their lives, Serena began to pack her belongings. She was pulling a cardboard box filled with her shoes into the hall when she backed right into Malcolm. With an "umf" she fell forward on the box.

"Come on, let me help you," he said, putting his hands onto her waist to help pull her up.

Serena's skin burned where his hands rested and

her nipples betrayed her and hardened into two tight aching buds.

Two weeks without Malcolm's sex and she was definitely going through withdrawal. Just last night she slept with a pillow between her legs.

Malcolm lifted her a little and set her down on her feet.

She turned to face him. "Thanks."

He looked down into the box, looking too fine in a white button-up shirt and vintage jeans. And the white looked divine against his bronzed complexion. "Packing already?" he asked.

"Yeah, might as well get it out the way, you know?" she said, putting her hands on her hips.

Malcolm's eyes darted down to her breasts pressing against the long-sleeved thermal shirt she wore and he quickly diverted his eyes as he felt things kicking to life below his belt. *Down boy*, he thought. "All of this will be over before we know it."

Yes, unfortunately so, Serena thought. "How are the interviews coming for the documentary?" she asked, changing the subject as she crossed her arms over her chest to hide her pebblelike nipples poking through the thin thermal.

Malcolm nodded. "Real good actually. And the salon?"

This polite strangerlike conversation was killing her, but Serena played along. "Great, just great. I um, I found two girls to rent booths and have been handing out flyers and doing promos on the radio. Trying to build up some hype, you know. I actually decided to hire an esthetician part-time and I'll see how it goes."

"Esthetician?"

"She'll do facials. No need having a nice hairdo and nasty skin, right?"

They fell silent.

"I better get going," Malcolm said, giving her one last look-over.

"All right, bye," she said, watching him as he walked down the stairs until his bald head disappeared from her view. She fanned herself with her hand and used two fingers to try to press her nipples back to normalcy.

She was tempted to get her one last taste of that man before they went their separate ways, which of course would be wrong. All she could do was ask the Lord to cool her off before she stripped naked and laid it out for him like a buffet!

Malcolm hoisted the last case of his precious digital equipment into the back of his SUV. He was just jogging up the stairs when Serena stepped out of the house carrying a big duffel bag. His heart was pained because he knew this would probably be the last time he would see his sexy ex-wife.

"You want me to get that for you?" he offered, looking up at her with his eyes squinted against the winter winds swirling around them.

"No, I have it. It's my last one," she said, moving past him on the stairs to set it in the open trunk of her car.

Malcolm walked through the house one final time, smiling as he ran his hand over the top of the island when he remembered Serena's striptease. It was going to take him some time to get her out of his system, that was for sure.

In the den, he walked up to the stately picture of his grandmother. He still couldn't believe she had been in love with Hamp all these years. He had told no one, not even his father, and definitely not Hamp. It wasn't his place. *Sorry your plan didn't work, Mama James*, he thought, knowing she could hear him.

A shimmer went across his body and he knew Serena was in the room with him. Turning, he smiled at her. "Well, we made it out alive, huh?"

Serena wrung her hands in front of her. "I wasn't sure that we would, but yeah, we made it," she agreed softly.

Their eyes locked and then they both looked away, speaking in unison.

"Serena—"

"Malcolm—"

They laughed a little.

"Ladies first," Malcolm told her.

"I just wanted to say that I'm glad we got through all that drama and that, um, we can be friendly again," she said.

Malcolm nodded as he licked his lips and forced a smile. "Yeah, me too."

They fell silent, neither ready to leave quite yet.

"I hope your father's friend takes good care of the house," Serena said, searching for something, *anything* to say, to stay in his presence for just a moment longer.

"I hope so, too, for his sake or he'll be out of here quick as I can say month-to-month lease," Malcolm joked.

Again the silence, a quick look into each other's eyes, and an even quicker look away.

"Well, I gotta go, my Dad wants me to stop by their house before I head back to New York," Malcolm said, moving across the room.

"Yeah, me too, I gotta go pick up my check from Hamp."

Malcolm came to a halt in front of Serena.

Her heart stopped as she tilted her head to look up at him.

Slowly he raised his hands and lightly captured her face in his grasp. He needed to feel those lips at least one last time.

Serena wanted that kiss just as much.

As he lowered his head, Serena tilted her chin up. Both their eyes closed as if in slow motion. And the first touch of their lips made them both shiver. Serena lifted her hand to lightly grasp his elbows as Malcolm deepened the kiss with a groan of hunger.

There in the entry of the den, Malcolm and Serena let all of the passion and desire they had for one another flow into that kiss.

And then, in what seemed an instant, it was over.

Malcolm kissed her lips briefly one last time, letting his head rest lightly atop hers for just a moment as he whispered, "Good-bye, Serena."

And just like that he was gone and she was left alone, free now to let her tears flow.

It took Serena nearly an hour before she looked presentable enough to head over to Hamp's. Her tears had her eyes slightly puffy and a little red, but she looked a helluva lot better than the crying mess she was before.

Serena smiled at the receptionist as she walked into Hamp's offices in her jeans and down coat. To think the last time she'd been there she had no idea her life would be changed so drastically and that was just two months ago.

"Mr. Tyler will see you now."

Serena closed the *Essence* magazine she was flipping through and followed the woman back into Hamp's office to find the elderly gentleman sitting behind his desk.

"Hello there, Hamp. How are you?" she said, smiling as he rose to come around his desk for a brief but warm hug.

"I'm good. How are you, though?" he asked with concern, those wise eyes taking in her red eyes.

"I'm okay," she said, moving to take a seat before his desk.

Hamp said nothing, instead moving over to an oil painting of Louis Armstrong. Behind the painting was a safe and Serena watched as he put in the combination and removed a large manila envelope, before moving back to his desk.

He reclaimed his seat and smiled at her in a fatherly fashion as he pushed the envelope across his desk toward her. "It's all yours little lady."

Serena accepted the manila envelope and folded it to shove into the satchel purse she had slung over her shoulder. "Thanks."

"You know although I didn't agree with Olivia's methods, I must admit I thought it would work," Hamp said, his eyes drifting over to a 5"x7" photo on his desk.

"Well, it did in a way. Malcolm and I aren't enemies anymore. We did get a chance to talk all that through and at least agree we both had some blame in our break-up."

Hamp remained silent.

Serena followed his line of vision and noticed it was a picture of Olivia that he was staring at, lost in thought. "You loved her, didn't you, Hamp?" she asked.

He looked over at Serena with denial already in his eyes. "She was my friend, but I—"

"You were in love with her," Serena stated softly, rather than asked.

Hamp smiled sadly. "Doesn't matter now does it?"

Serena rose. "I have something you need to see," she said. "Be right back."

She made her way out of his office and then out of the building quicker than a roach fleeing light. She went in her car and dug around in her bags until she found the letter buried inside her business folder.

With it clutched in her hand, she jogged back into the building, passing by the receptionist to enter Hamp's office. With a huge grin, she handed him the letter without a second thought.

He looked at it and recognized it immediately. "No," he said adamantly. "Whatever is in there you are not to discuss it or show anyone."

"I'll just leave this here and you can do with it as you please," Serena said, setting the letter on his desk before she quietly left the office.

Hamp reached for his spectacles. He hadn't gotten to be a successful lawyer without drawing conclusions. Obviously there was something in that letter about him.

Quietly, he opened the envelope and unfolded the letter with his wrinkled fingers. He read it once, then twice, the entire time his heart soaring to read that his Olivia had loved him as well.

Chapter 15

One Year Later

"Haiba Day Spa & Salon. Please hold."

Serena pushed the HOLD button on the multiline phone system and then motioned for her receptionist to stop chatting with the shampoo girl and come do her job answering the phones and making appointments for Serena's booming business.

Her dreams were fulfilled. She had her own steady clientele, having procured a lot of her regulars from her Hair Happenings days. The two girls she hired straight out of cosmetology school also had their own following now. They all worked hard, but had fun, all the while keeping things professional the way Serena demanded. She had since hired on the esthetician three days a week and had converted the upstairs to a massage area that stayed booked during the two days a week the masseuse worked.

She was thinking of hiring them both on five days a week and offering some spa packages and upgrading the services a bit. She definitely had enough profit to do it.

She looked around at the soothing natural colors

of the décor and thought it looked like a New York day spa. That plus their skill at delivering original hairdos, as well as professional consultations—because every hairstyle didn't fit every face—had them packed six days a week. Yes, they were open on Mondays. She alternated the scheduling so that everyone got their two days off a week.

Serena had even procured a salon spotlight in most of the major hair magazines as well as *Essence*. It was all about publicity, publicity, publicity.

Serena was glad she had her business because her love life was definitely on the rocks. In the year since she had last seen Malcolm, she had tried dating on two occasions and failed at it miserably. Neither man could compete and so she lost interest quickly. She doubted if she would ever truly get Malcolm out of her system.

Malcolm entered his loft, running his hand over the sensor to bathe the space with light. He bent over, his hands on his knees as he breathed slowly. He had just completed a five-mile run in Central Park and his lungs felt like they were on fire. Moving to the kitchen he grabbed a bottle of water, which he nearly drank in one full gulp, tilting his bald head back.

Tossing the bottle into the trash, he began to strip off his clothing. He was gloriously naked when he reached his bedroom. He strode into the state of the art bathroom and turned the shower on full blast, letting the steam coat the glass walls and mirrors before he climbed in and sat down on the marble bench, letting the water shower down on him.

He tilted his head back, enjoying the feel of the water pelting against his face.

In just three days it would be Christmas, and Malcolm was in a bah-humbug-type of mood. His father and Elaine wanted him to drive into Jersey and spend the holiday with them. His friends wanted to spend the weekend skiing. He wasn't particularly interested in doing either.

This time last year he had kissed Serena for the last time and it was a kiss that seared his soul and was branded into his memory, even more so than the steamy night they'd shared when he proclaimed his love for her.

He missed her still. He wanted her still. He loved her still.

Standing, he reached for his soap and wash cloth and scrubbed the sweat and grime from his body, as he symbolically tried his best to scrub Serena from his thoughts.

Last Christmas had been awful. He had been fresh off of Serena's rejection and not yet ready to be around his family and friends. He spent the day drinking beers and hoping Serena was as miserable as he was.

Malcolm turned off the shower and grabbed a towel to wrap low around his waist. How many times over the year had he started to call her? To say 'Merry Christmas?' Or 'Happy Birthday?' To say 'Congratulations on your Grand Opening?' To say 'Good job on the write up in *Essence*?'

Each time he got as far as dialing the sixth digit after the area code he would hang up. *Move on*, he would admonish himself.

And he tried. He dated often, but he found himself comparing the women to Serena and each and every time for whatever reason the women came up lacking. Each woman was just a reminder that it was Serena he wanted in his life.

He had to do something, sitting around moping

all holiday when he could either try his hand at skiing for the first time or indulge in Elaine's good cooking and his father's fried turkey was not the answer.

He weighed the two and decided that fried turkey won out over freezing on a ski slope. *Jersey it is.*

Luther shoved his lit cigar in his mouth, zipped up his overcoat and stepped outside in the dead of winter to check on his turkey frying away in the backyard.

"Luther Saint James, you gone catch your death worrying 'bout that bird in all that snow," Elaine hollered to him out the kitchen window, before slamming it shut.

She could say what she pleased but there was nothing better then a fried turkey on Christmas. Now of course he wished it was safe enough to fry in the house but any fool knew this was an outdoor thing, a man's thing, and he was going to have his fried turkey. No cold weather, nagging wife, or late-to-show son was gonna stop him.

Luther rolled his cigar around from one side of his mouth to the other and looked down at his watch. Malcolm had called hours ago to say he was on his way. He should have arrived by now.

He had just lowered the lid on his oversized turkey pot when the phone rang. A chill ran straight through his bones. The older folks said a chill like that meant someone was walking over your grave.

"Luther!" Elaine yelled out, swinging the back door open wide.

At the look on her face his heart stopped.

"Luther turn that pot off. We got to go baby. It's Malcolm. He's been in an accident."

Luther's cigar fell from his mouth and hit the snow with a hiss.

Serena pulled the pan of her Auntie's dressing from the oven and set it on the counter with a proud smile. Her *Soulful Christmas* CD was blaring as Al Green tore up "Silent Night" like only Al could. Her live tree was decorated to the hilt with every decoration she could squeeze onto it and spiked eggnog was chilling in the fridge.

She was forcing herself into the holiday spirit. It was Christmas and she was going to have a good time if it killed her.

Still, nothing like the holidays to make you realize just how much you wanted a man and some babies in your life.

Elaine had offered for her to come have dinner with them, but Serena declined. That's all she needed was to be sitting there only the lonely when Malcolm walked in with some beauty on his arm.

And one of the girls from the salon was having a big bash at her house and Serena told her she might drop by, but in truth she planned to pig out on dressing and get buzzed off eggnog until both put her to sleep and she didn't wake until Christmas was over.

Serena was just dumping a large helping of her dressing onto a plate when her phone rang. Dancing around to the Jackson Five's rendition of "Santa Claus is Coming to Town," Serena made her way to pick up her cordless phone from the top of the fridge. "Merry Christmas and Happy early Kwanzaa," she sang into the phone with cheerful eyes.

Moments later, those eyes went dull, and everything in her hands went crashing to the floor as she frantically grabbed her car keys and coat before she flew out of the house.

Luther sat by his son's side, his expression grave as he held his hand and tried to will him back to consciousness. "Come on, son," he whispered to him. "Don't you leave me."

He didn't get a response. Malcolm was unconscious and the doctors weren't sure when, or if, he would regain consciousness.

Luther leaned forward and pressed his lips to his sons flaccid hand. Tears filled his eyes.

Serena got to University Medical Center on Bergen Street in record time, barely parking her car before she raced into the emergency room.

She stopped at the nurse's station, her chest heaving from the exertion and her fear. "Malcolm Saint James, please."

The portly nurse looked up. "Are you a relative?" she asked.

"I'm his wife, Serena. Serena Saint James," she lied with ease.

The nurse gave her directions to Malcolm's room in the Intensive Care Unit. Serena opened the door with trepidation and at her first sight of him, her skin blanched and she felt her knees weaken. "Oh, Malcolm," she wailed softly, not even seeing Luther and Elaine as she moved to his side and bent to press her face close to his.

He was still. Too still. Deathly still.

"Serena."

She looked up with eyes dazed with pain and finally saw Luther and Elaine looking at her with concern.

"What happened to him?" she asked, still holding his hand tightly.

"He was hit head-on by a stolen car on Frelinghuysen Avenue on his way to our house for Christmas dinner," Elaine answered, as Luther shut his eyes and covered his face with his cap. "They had to cut him out of the car."

Serena nodded but she was numb as she looked down into Malcolm's battered and bruised face. She leaned down and whispered in his ear. "I'm here, Malcolm and I swear, I won't leave your side until you wake up and smile at me. You hear me?"

Elaine came close to the bed to pick up her husband's hand and reach across Malcolm's prone legs for Serena's free hand. She clasped them both tightly and bowed her head. "Heavenly father . . ."

Even after Malcolm's condition stabilized and they moved him to a private room, Serena remained in a chair by Malcolm's side for the next three days and three nights. She held his hand, she gave him his sponge baths, she talked to him about their past, she willed him to open those beautiful eyes and look up at her. She told him over and over just how much she loved him and how foolish she'd been for not taking that chance on their love.

She was rubbing his hand and recalling the first time they met, when the door opened and Luther walked in carrying a small bag she recognized.

"Elaine went by your place and packed you a bag. If you ain't gone go home at least take you a shower here and change out of them clothes."

"I guess I do stink," she said with a smile that didn't reach her eyes. "And Lord knows my mouth tastes like somebody's funky feet."

"I'll sit with him. Go on and freshen up."

Serena accepted the bag and carried it into the bathroom. Not wanting to be away from Malcolm's side for too long, she took a quick shower, got rid of the funk on her breath, and changed into a velour sweat suit and footie socks. As she wiped the steam from the small mirror above the sink with the side of her hand, she was shocked by how haggard she looked, especially with her weave a tangled bird's nest on her head. Using her fingers she tried her best to remove the tangles before she brushed it back into a tight ponytail at the base of her neck.

When she walked back into the room, Elaine had joined them and was removing Tupperware from a plastic bag. When Elaine saw her she walked over and kissed Serena's cheek as she rubbed her arm affectionately. "You look like yourself again. Now sit down and eat some of this turkey soup I brought you."

Serena reclaimed her seat by Malcolm, entwining her hands with his. "I'm not really hungry," she protested.

Elaine shifted Malcolm's table to sit it in front of Serena and lowered it to set her bowl and a spoon atop of it. "Eat," she ordered, reminding Serena of Auntie.

And she did eat, but she held onto Malcolm with one hand and scooped her soup with the other.

Serena gave in to her exhaustion and fell asleep in the chair with her head resting on the edge of Malcolm's bed. Feeling stiff she released Malcolm's hand and stretched her limbs like a lazy cat.

"Thought you promised not to let my hand go."

Serena gasped in surprise and looked over to see Malcolm's eyes open and resting on her. She grasped his hand with both of hers and held it to her heart as she bent over and pressed her lips to his with all of the love she had in her. "Thank you, Jesus," she whispered, as she put feather-light kisses over his face.

"I'm going to get the nurse," Serena told him. But his grasp on her hand stopped her and she looked at him.

"You know I'm going to hold you to everything you've been saying to me," Malcolm told her, wincing slightly.

"And you should because I meant every word. I love you, Malcolm Saint James, and I don't ever want to live my life without you in it," she promised him, as she bent again to taste those lips she loved.

"You already know I love you, right?"

Serena nodded. "Yes, I do."

Malcolm began to chuckle.

"What's so funny?" she asked.

He nodded his chin towards his feet and Serena followed his line of vision, her mouth gaping as she saw his thin blanket tented by his erection.

They both laughed quietly as they waited for his erection to ease before she called in the hospital staff.

"You're insatiable," she scolded him playfully.

"And you love it."

Serena winked at him. "Damn right I do."

Epilogue

Serena smiled slowly and stretched her limbs as her husband's large hands continued to rub cocoa butter across her belly, now swollen with six months of pregnancy. "Ah, you spoil me," she sighed as she turned her head on the pillow to look at her handsome husband stretched out on his side beside her on the queen-sized bed.

Malcolm winked at her as he moved one of his hands to slip beneath her shirt to caress one full breast. "I love when you're pregnant," he said honestly, scooting closer on the bed to take one dark chocolate aureole into his mouth. He lightly flicked the nipple with his tongue.

Serena moaned in pleasure, allowing herself to enjoy his skill for just a few precious moments before she playfully swatted the back of his bald head. "Baby, let's not start something we can't finish," she said, already breathing heavy and not quite meaning her words.

Malcolm deepened his sucking motion, drawing more of her breast into his mouth and his member ached to be inside of her.

"Whoo! Lord Jesus," she gasped, actually raising a

hand to fan herself. "Luther and Elaine will be here any minute—"

Ding-dong.

"Damn," they swore in unison, their bodies reluctantly drifting apart.

Malcolm rolled off the bed trying to arrange the oversized football jersey and jeans he wore to hide his erection. "I'll go down."

She heard his feet thunder against the steps as she rose from the bed relatively easily. Thankfully, the pregnancy had not yet encumbered her movement.

As she pushed her feet into her favorite fluffy slippers, she looked around the room. Once it had been filled with the lace and ruffles Mama James preferred. Now it was decorated in neutral tones with a contemporary fashion that suited both Malcolm and Serena's style.

After his car accident, they both decided not to waste any more time apart. So Malcom gave his renters in Mama James' house ninety days' notice and moved in with Serena in the interim. During that time, they planned their second wedding, put his loft up for sale, and moved his offices to downtown Newark, while he finished *Hip-Hop Domination*—for which he eventually won his second Emmy Award.

In no time at all they had a beautiful summer wedding in the backyard—again, and began their second chance at love where it all started. Neither could wait for their own children to enjoy growing up in the same neighborhood where they discovered each other first as best friends and then lovers.

That was five years ago, and Serena felt blessed that Mama James played that hand in throwing them back together. The love and commitment they shared now would have been lost to them forever without her.

Thank the heavens for Mama James, Serena thought.

She had just shifted to sit up in bed when Malcom walked into their bedroom with their three-year-old daughter Aliana on his hip.

Her family.

With a protective hand on her belly, Serena smiled at them both with all the love she had in her heart for them.

Dear Readers,

Thanks for reading Serena and Malcolm's story, which followed their love from childhood to adulthood, from the great, the bad and the great again as they fought hard for a love that could not be denied.

Next up is *You Never Know*. This is a anthology I'm working on with Melanie Schuster and Kimberley White so you all know it's gonna be HOT, HOT, HOT!!! That's up for spring of 2006.

Again I thank all of my wonderful readers for your support and your dedication to these wonderful, sometimes crazy, characters of mine. I have the best readers ever and I appreciate each and every one of you for all of the wonderful love and support you have shown over the years.

My special thanks to the over 125 members of my online book club, Niobia_Bryant_News. Thank you all times a million.

Back to my office.

Blessings ya'll,

Niobia

ABOUT THE AUTHOR

Niobia Simone Bryant has taken the romance world by storm since her 2000 release of *Admission of Love*. With national best-selling status, award wins, and four critically acclaimed releases under her belt, she truly believes the best is yet to come.

When she's not tied to her computer, she loves cooking, reading all genres of literature, and spending time with boyfriend, family, and friends.

For more on this author who cannot be stopped, go to her website: *www.geocities.com/niobia_bryant*, where you can also join her free online book club Niobia_Bryant_News. Or you can email her at *Niobia_Bryant@yahoo.com*.